TO CATCH A
CHEAT

VARIAN JOHNSON

SCHOLASTIC INC.

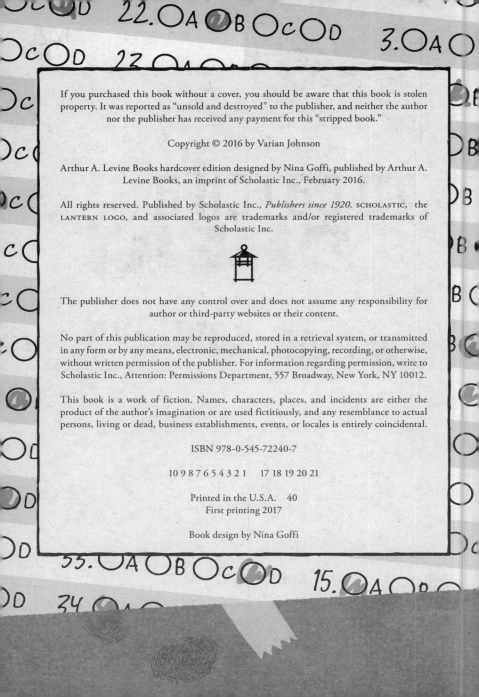

Copyright © 2016 by Varian Johnson

Arthur A. Levine Books hardcover edition designed by Nina Goffi, published by Arthur A. Levine Books, an imprint of Scholastic Inc., February 2016.

ISBN 978-0-545-72240-7

10 9 8 7 6 5 4 3 2 1   17 18 19 20 21

Printed in the U.S.A.   40
First printing 2017

Book design by Nina Goffi

FOR **SYDNEY**.
WELCOME TO THE CREW.

CAST

Gang Greene

Jackson Greene — con artist (reformed)

Charlie De La Cruz — editor of the *Maplewood Herald*

Megan Feldman — president of the Tech Club

Hashemi Larijani — member of the Tech Club; inventor

Bradley Boardman — Art Geek; guidance office helper

Other Students

Gabriela De La Cruz — president of the Maplewood Middle School
    Student Council; basketball player

Rob Richards — Jackson's American history classmate

Thom Jordan — Jackson's American history classmate

Lynne Thurber — basketball player

Keith Sinclair — basketball player; disgraced ex-candidate for
    Maplewood Student Council president

Wilton Jones — member of the Environmental Action Team

Carmen Cleaver — member of the Environmental Action Team

Victor Cho — former Chess Team member

Lincoln Miller — chair of the Maplewood Honor Board

Serena Bianchi — member of the Maplewood Honor Board

Kayla Hall — president of the Riggins Middle School Robotics Club

Eric Caan — Riggins Middle School student

Adults

MRS. CLARK — legendarily tough teacher of American history

DR. KELSEY — principal of Maplewood Middle School

MR. JAMES — security guard

MR. HUTTON — custodian

COACH RAINEY — Maplewood girls' basketball coach

SAMUEL GREENE — Jackson's older brother; freshman at the University
of Pennsylvania

RAY BASILONE — locksmith at Basilone's Lock and Key; Samuel's friend

a TEST OF WILLS

Jackson Greene placed his pen on his desk, loosened his red tie, then flipped the page on his American history exam. It was only a practice test, but Mrs. Clark had promised that any student who scored above 95 percent would automatically be excused from her brutal end-of-the semester final. That was supposed to serve as an incentive for students to study over the winter break.

Given the moans, groans, and grunts echoing around the room, Jackson guessed that everyone would be taking the final exam. Including him.

He had just reached question forty-one out of fifty when Becca Simpson, the first period office helper, entered the room and handed Mrs. Clark a note.

"I'm sorry," the teacher said to Becca after she had switched on a desk lamp to read the message, "but the principal will have to wait until Jackson finishes his exam." Her eyes locked on to Jackson. "Eyes on your desk, Mr. Greene!"

Jackson sighed and returned to his exam as the office

helper left the room. Of course Dr. Kelsey wanted to see him — Jackson was always his number-one suspect when something went wrong at the school. Still, it would have been nice to go at least one full day after returning from winter break without seeing the principal.

A few minutes later, the timer on the teacher's desk buzzed.

Rob Richards slammed down his pen. "Forty minutes already?" He turned to his best friend, Thom Jordan. "I was sure we had —"

"No talking!" Mrs. Clark said, crossing her arms. "Or do you two need another reminder of my rules?"

"No, ma'am," both Rob and Thom mumbled.

Jackson shook his head. Sneaking a glance at Mrs. Clark was one thing, but *talking* during one of her exams? No way. The rumor was, the last time someone spoke during a test, she ripped the student's paper in half and kicked him out of the room.

Mrs. Clark passed through the rows of students, picking up each test and pen. She locked everything up in her file cabinet and slipped the ring of keys into her pocket.

"The final exam is in less than two weeks. Given the answers I saw as I walked around the room, I'd suggest you start studying *now*." She made her way to the front of the class. "Everyone turn to page eighty-five in the text. Except you, Mr. Greene," she said. "You're wanted in the main office."

Jackson grabbed his book bag and glanced at Hashemi Larijani, who sat a few seats behind him. Hashemi offered him a sympathetic look before turning back to his desk.

Jackson walked down the hallway, his feet making squishing sounds on the still-wet carpet. All the toilets in the school had flooded over the weekend, ruining the carpeting in half of the building. Some kids were calling it an accident, but Jackson knew a prank when he saw one.

Which was why he figured Dr. Kelsey wanted to see him.

Ever since the Election Job — or as Hashemi and the others still called it, the Great Greene Heist — Dr. Kelsey had made it his mission to catch Jackson in the act of another con. But there was nothing for Kelsey to catch. The crew had disbanded. Gang Greene was no more, and the Infamous Jackson Greene had retired.

Allegedly.

Plus, stopping Keith Sinclair from winning a rigged election had been an act performed in the name of justice. Flooding the bathrooms was a whole different type of prank — destructive and stupid. There was no way he'd pull a pointless stunt like that, not when things were going so well between him and Gaby. As Student Council president, she took matters like school vandalism very seriously.

Jackson entered the atrium just as his best friend and Gaby's twin brother, Charlie de la Cruz, exited the main office. "Hey, Charlie," Jackson said. "Did Kelsey call you in about the flooding?"

"Of course," Charlie said, crossing his arms. "Why wouldn't he?"

Jackson frowned. "You almost sound like you *wanted* to be questioned."

"I'm just saying — I could pull that prank just as well as you could."

"What? Charlie, I never said —"

"Forget it," Charlie said, walking away. "Better hurry. Don't want to keep Kelsey waiting."

Before Jackson could process Charlie's attitude, the office door swung open. "Mr. Greene," Dr. Kelsey boomed. "Cut the chatter and get in here. We have a lot to discuss."

Jackson followed Dr. Kelsey into his office, then covered his nose. Something smelled reminiscent of his father's liver-and-onion casserole. "I think there's a dead animal in here," he said.

"You're full of jokes, aren't you, Mr. Greene." The principal settled behind his desk and nodded toward a pair of brown loafers in the corner. "I ruined those running into the boys' bathroom. By that point, the toilets had already flooded most of the social studies hallway." He steepled his fingers. "But enough about my shoes. Tell me, where were you on Saturday evening?"

Jackson sat down on the other side of the desk. "Saturday? Mr. James said the prank happened on Sunday."

"Mr. James should focus on security, not plumbing," Dr. Kelsey replied. "No, given the amount of damage, we suspect that the toilets were clogged on Saturday evening, after the boys' basketball practice. The faucets were turned on as well. So I'll ask again — where were you on Saturday between five and eight o'clock?"

"At the library. Studying." Jackson focused on Dr. Kelsey's nose. He told himself not to blink, not to hesitate. "My dad dropped me off. I checked out books and everything."

"Did anyone else see you there?"

"I don't know. Maybe."

"Then you don't have an alibi."

"But I just said —"

"Let's be honest. A boy with your particular talents wouldn't have any problem sneaking out of a public library unnoticed." Dr. Kelsey pulled a black messenger bag from his bottom file cabinet. "We found this wedged behind a door. Do you recognize it?"

"I think I saw it at Target," Jackson said. "Or maybe Walmart. On clearance. You know I'm a sucker for sales."

"Mr. Greene, I've been very lenient with you over the last few months. I would hate to go back to our weekly meetings and random locker searches."

Jackson glanced at the bag again. The flap was decorated with stickers from *Rights of Warfare: Southern Seas*. "Just because it looks like Charlie's bag doesn't mean it's his."

"It gets better." Dr. Kelsey pulled a small notebook from the bag. The letters *JG* were stenciled into its red leather cover. "Recognize this?"

"I've never seen that notebook before."

Dr. Kelsey flipped it open. "Are you sure? It looks a lot like your handwriting."

Jackson squinted at the notebook. He didn't want to admit it, but Kelsey was right. From what he could see, the writing even matched his standard coding system, though none of the notes made sense. "Anyone could have copied my handwriting," he said.

"Admit it. You got sloppy. You got caught."

"But I didn't do it!"

"Last chance, Mr. Greene," the principal said, clearly enjoying himself. "You were fortunate enough to avoid getting caught during the fiasco with the Student Council election a few months ago, but your luck will eventually run out. If you confess now, I'll give you only a five-day suspension." He returned the notebook and bag to the drawer. "I won't be so forgiving later."

Jackson chewed on his lip. Kelsey was bluffing. He *had* to be. There was no way he could suspend him for that long without proof. "What about the security system?" he finally asked. "Check the NVR."

Dr. Kelsey pounced. "And how do you know the security system uses a network video recorder?"

"Dr. Kelsey, *all* modern security systems use NVRs." He had actually heard about Dr. Kelsey's new super hi-tech NVR and sixteen-camera surveillance system from a number of people — Mr. James, the security guard; Megan Feldman, tech geek / part-time con artist / seventh period office helper / ex-cheerleader; and even Lincoln Miller, the Student Honor Board chairman. But as tempting as it was, beyond noting the locations of the new cameras, Jackson didn't bother to learn much about the system. He figured he had no need — he really was trying to stay retired.

"I bet you could even stream video from the NVR to your computer," Jackson continued. "Go ahead. Look at it. That'll prove I didn't pull the prank."

"I can't. Someone stole the hard drive from the NVR," Dr. Kelsey said. "I'm sure you're going to say that you didn't have anything to do with that either."

"Of course I didn't," Jackson said. "But I'm guessing you've already checked my locker to be sure."

"You're still on probation, Mr. Greene. I can check your person or belongings whenever I wish."

Jackson's long brown fingers tightened on the chair's armrests. Mr. James had also mentioned that each camera contained a small amount of flash memory. It was meant to serve as a backup in case the NVR hard drive was corrupted. Or stolen.

Jackson took a deep breath. "Isn't there some type of backup?" he asked. "Like, maybe the cameras somehow —"

"Save the effort, Mr. Greene," Dr. Kelsey said. "I know you snuck in on Saturday because the cameras hold only twenty-four hours of video. Then they record over the previous day's data. You knew any trace of your break-in would be gone by Monday morning."

Actually, he hadn't known all of that. Jackson was tempted to pull out his notebook, just so he could capture all the facts. "Dr. Kelsey, I promise — I didn't pull this prank."

Dr. Kelsey grinned. No, he *smirked*. "That's fine. You don't have to talk. I'm sure I can eventually convince Charlie de la Cruz to speak up. Or maybe I'll chat with Hashemi Larijani. Or Charlie's new best friend, Bradley Boardman. It's funny how students start talking once you take away their perks."

"They didn't have anything to do with this."

"And you did?" Dr. Kelsey's face stiffened. "Last chance. If you don't confess now, your potential suspension goes up to ten days. I'll also bar you from participating in all school activities and field trips for the rest of the year. The Botany Club, the class trip to Cedar Point, the Spring Formal — everything."

Jackson straightened his tie. This was pointless. As far as Dr. Kelsey was concerned, he was guilty. He was sure the principal would march him in front of the Honor Board today if he could. And Jackson couldn't tell him what he'd actually been doing Saturday night — not without getting Gaby in trouble too.

It was time to bring in the big guns.

"Can I use the phone?" Jackson asked, already sliding forward in his chair. "I need to call my dad."

SENDING A MESSAGE

Gabriela de la Cruz sat in the computer lab on Monday afternoon, her ponytail curled around her finger, and reread her draft email to the teachers about February's school-wide community service project. Satisfied, she hit SEND, then refreshed her inbox.

No new messages.

She checked her phone as well, then rose from her desk and walked to the window. It provided a bird's-eye view of the entire northeast side of campus, including the school's garden. One member of the Botany Club stood in the snow, spreading mulch around the base of the peony plants.

She shut down her computer and headed outside. She had to lean into the wind as she walked.

"It's days like this that I really wish you had a cell phone," Gaby said once she reached the garden. "It would have been a lot easier to text you instead of coming out here."

Jackson offered her a small smile. "At this rate, my parents will never buy me a phone. I'd be better off asking Hash to build me one."

9

"Are they mad?"

"No, but still . . . Dad doesn't exactly enjoy getting calls at work about me." He returned the almost-empty sack of mulch to the toolshed. "What about your parents? Do they believe Charlie?"

"I don't know. I didn't have a chance to talk to him for very long. He swears that he didn't do it, but the only alibi he has for that night is hanging out with Bradley. Which doesn't help."

Jackson scuffed the bottom of his shoe against the hard ground, knocking dirty snow from his soles. "I heard your practice was canceled." He leaned against the fence. "Want to bike over to the Fitz and shoot some hoops?"

"I'm not in the mood for basketball today." Gaby leaned against the fence as well. Her arm pressed against Jackson's, but given their heavy coats, she wondered if it really counted as contact. "You could come over to my house. My dad is making tortilla soup."

"Yeah, and I bet my bowl will get a cup of diced jala-peños. Or some bleach."

"How many times do I have to tell you? Daddy likes you."

"*Liked.* Ever since I . . . Ever since we . . ." Jackson shook his head. "The last time I was there, he was sharpening his Rambo knife."

"He was just playing with you."

"I guess I missed the joke." He shifted closer to her. "Since when do you not want to play basketball?" he asked. "Don't say it's because of the snow. We've played in worse weather."

"I'm just worried about Charlie," she said. "He's been really antsy for the past two weeks. Fidgety. Like he always gets —"

"When he's planning a job," Jackson said.

She nodded. "If he really did it . . ." She let her words die away as the wind picked up. A few strands of hair fell into her face, but she didn't bother brushing them off. She hadn't come out here to talk about Charlie. Not really.

She had spent the past few hours trying to figure out what to say to Jackson about Saturday night, but now that she was here, nothing sounded good enough. Finally, she blurted, "I'm sorry."

"For what?"

Gaby shielded her eyes with her hand. The sun was shining off the snow, turning the ground extremely bright. Plus, this way, she didn't have to look directly at him. "If it weren't for me, you wouldn't be in this mess."

"How? Even if I had been studying in the library, I wouldn't have had an alibi," Jackson said. "Lynne said her brother needed your help. It's what friends do."

Lynne Thurber's younger brother, a fourth grader at Gardner Elementary, had lost all his birthday money in a lopsided pickup football game with some boys from Riggins Middle School. Lucky for Lynne, her best friend's pseudo-boyfriend excelled in retrieving misappropriated items.

"You could just tell Dr. Kelsey that we were scamming Eric Caan and his friends out of their money and video games," she said. "There's your alibi right there."

"I'm guessing that wouldn't go over so well with either of our parents."

"But you wouldn't be facing suspension."

"No, I'd just be grounded for the rest of the year. Not exactly apples for apples, but close." He coughed. "I don't want to miss the Spring Formal."

"The formal isn't until May."

Jackson grinned. "I'm planning ahead."

The wind whipped up again, and they both shivered. It was times like this that Jackson wished he really *were* Gaby's boyfriend, because he was sure that a boyfriend would know what to do when his girlfriend was cold. Was he supposed to offer her his coat, even though she was already wearing one? His gloves? Was he supposed to wrap his arms around her to keep her warm?

"I should go," she said, pushing off the fence. "Mom and Dad are going to want me home early today."

Jackson followed her out of the gate, though she was walking much faster than he. He had hoped working in the garden would help clear his mind — help him sort out the facts of the prank. See the angles. But he remained as confused as before, if not more so.

But there *was* one pattern. . . . A lack of alibis for all his friends.

Gaby stopped in front of the school and waited for Jackson to catch up. "What's going on in that head of yours? The Infamous Jackson Greene is not known for walking so slowly. Especially in weather like this."

That made him laugh a little. "It's just . . . I don't have

a legitimate alibi, and neither do Charlie and Bradley. If Hash and Megan don't have one either . . ."

"What? You think someone's trying to frame you guys?"

"Maybe," he said. "When you go home, can you poke around and see if you can find Charlie's messenger bag?"

"Sure. Why?"

"Kelsey found one at the scene. It may not be Charlie's, but it sure looked like it. It even held this expensive-looking notebook with what looked like my handwriting."

Gaby grabbed Jackson's hand. "There was a notebook?"

"Yeah. Leather, with my initials stenciled on the front."

"Red leather? With gold stenciling?"

Jackson nodded.

"That thief!" She tightened her grip around Jackson's fingers. "That was part of your Christmas gift — it was supposed to go with the tie I bought you. I lost it a few weeks ago, and thought I'd misplaced it in my room. I figured I'd give it to you for your birthday next month." Gaby looked down at their hands pressed together and quickly returned hers to her pockets. "Sorry. I didn't mean . . ."

"No, it's okay," Jackson said, flexing his fingers. "But now I'm wondering if I need to upgrade *your* birthday present." Hers was in two weeks, on the Monday after the American history exam. He hadn't even thought about Charlie's gift yet.

"You just found out that Charlie stole your gift — a gift that somehow ended up at the scene of a crime — and you're worried about *my* birthday present?"

Jackson pictured the Ruth Bader Ginsburg Chia Pet hidden underneath his bed. "Believe me, if you knew what I bought you, you'd want me to upgrade."

She let out a long stream of air. "Boys . . ."

"Do me a favor," Jackson said. "Don't talk to Charlie about the notebook yet. I want to check a few sources first." He paused while a few students passed. "Hash and Megan will be tied up in Tech Club for another couple of hours. That'll give me plenty of time to scope out Hash's shed. If they've been up to something, I'll find answers there."

Gaby crossed her arms. "Please don't tell me you're going to break into his shed."

"Well, it's not like I haven't done it before."

"But you promised Hashemi that you'd stop," Gaby said. "You promised *me*."

Jackson rubbed the back of his neck. "How else am I supposed to figure out what's going on?"

"You could open that mouth of yours and talk to them. They're your friends after all."

"Tell that to your brother."

"What happened between you two?"

"Nothing. He just seemed weird when I saw him earlier. Like he was angry at me."

Gaby hesitated, then said, "Dr. Kelsey tried to get Charlie to pin the prank on you. He promised that he'd go easy on Charlie — since, he said, there was no way Charlie could have pulled it off without you."

"Wow, that explains why he was so mad in the hallway." Jackson shrugged. "Though Kelsey's got a point."

"Jackson . . ."

"We both know that planning jobs isn't Charlie's strength. Remember the last time he tried to run a job without me? He had diarrhea for a week." Jackson pulled a small tin of mints from his pocket. "Want one? Only two left."

Gaby's face reddened. As she took a mint, Jackson realized that he was sending the wrong message. He just needed an empty tin. He wasn't trying to kiss Gaby.

Well, technically, he wasn't trying to kiss Gaby *today*. At school. In thirty-degree weather. After he'd eaten a chili-cheese hot dog for lunch.

But then again . . . They were alone. Maybe . . .

He shook his head. His brother's Rules of Romance said that a first kiss was supposed to be romantic and memorable, and this situation was anything but.

Jackson popped his mint into his mouth, then started talking again to fill the silence. "All I know is, it's too much of a coincidence that neither Charlie nor I have alibis," he said. "Eric Caan insisted we meet on Saturday night. Maybe it was all staged." He sighed. "No, that's crazy."

"And expensive," Gaby said. "Who *wants* to lose a bunch of money and video games?" Her phone beeped in her back pocket. "Shoot. That's probably Dad." She pulled out her phone and pressed a few buttons. Then her hand flew to her mouth.

"What's wrong?" he asked. "Is it your parents?"

"No. It's a message." She showed him the phone. "For you."

THE MORE THINGS **CHANGE**

Megan pulled her coat closer to her body as she and Hashemi walked to his house. They hadn't spoken since leaving the Tech Club meeting, but if they were going to have any hope of completing the RhinoBot in time for the Battle of the Robots competition, they'd have to come to an agreement soon.

Or rather, they'd have to finally get something out of beta.

She started to touch his arm to get his attention but pulled back at the last second. Megan knew Hashemi still had a bit of a crush on her, and she didn't want to do anything to lead him on. She liked him a lot — he was the smartest guy she knew — but after the fiasco with Stewart Hogan at the beginning of the school year, she wasn't in the mood for boys. Besides, she hadn't quit cheerleading for romance.

Megan waited until they reached the gate to his backyard before clearing her throat. "Hashemi," she said. "I know you want to keep making improvements to the

RhinoBot, but we're running out of time. The competition is three weeks away."

"I know." He knocked some snow off the gate, then opened it. "But you have to admit, adding a steel-plated pneumatic battering ram to its snout is a good idea. Much better than just a plain horn."

"How many times do we have to discuss this? The battery can't handle it," she said. "It can barely power a light bulb."

"You know, I've been reconsidering —"

"No."

"But, Megan —"

"You're not going to build a battery from scratch again. The RhinoBot went haywire last time." She followed him through the gate. "I lost half of my Christmas money thanks to you."

"I really am sorry about your mother's china cabinet —"

"And you fried the motor. And melted the motherboard."

He winced. "Yes, all true. But technically, the battery worked."

"For five minutes!" She shook her head. "The worst thing is, now we're stuck working in the dungeon again."

"Home sweet home." Hashemi readjusted his glasses. "Perhaps there's a way to squeeze a little more juice out of the operating system."

"I've tried," she said. She had built a custom Linux-based operating system just to eke out as much battery life as possible. "Though I might save a few amps by cutting those voice-operated commands you asked me to include. . . ."

"No, you're correct. The OS is perfect as is." He continued toward the back of the house. "Just give me two more days. I'm sure I can come up with something —"

Hashemi stopped so abruptly, Megan almost collided with him. "What's wrong?"

She followed his gaze to the shed, where Jackson Greene sat on a milk crate outside the door.

"I was wondering if you guys would ever show up," Jackson said as he put away his notebook. "I've been here for ten minutes, and I'm starting to lose the feeling in my toes."

Hashemi took a deep breath. Charlie had already updated him and Megan on his conversation with Dr. Kelsey and warned them that Jackson might pay them a visit. But as long as they didn't admit anything, they figured they'd be okay. Surely if they could design a rhinoceros-shaped robot with a battering ram (and questionable battery life), they could handle a brief conversation with Jackson Greene.

Jackson rose from the crate. "The competition's at the end of the month, right?"

"Three weeks," Megan said.

"But we'll be ready," Hashemi added. "We just have a few final improvements to make. Tweaks, really."

Jackson laughed. "Good to know some things don't change." He straightened his tie. "Got a few minutes to talk?"

Megan and Hashemi looked at each other. She

shrugged, then said, "I'm surprised you didn't pick the lock and wait inside the shed."

"I was tempted." Jackson opened a small mint tin. Inside was a bed of gray clay imprinted with a key shape. "I broke into Hash's locker at school and made a mold of the shed key."

Hashemi shook his head. "Jackson, you promised —"

"Which is why I didn't use it." Jackson offered him the tin and a clear plastic key. "I really am retired. Mostly."

Hashemi weighed the key in the palm of his hand. "What is this made of? Silicone?"

"It's a high-strength epoxy polymer," Jackson replied. "Dries faster than silicone. Twice as strong."

"Let me be clear: It was wrong for you to break into my locker — but this key *is* kind of cool." Hashemi handed the key to Megan. "Do you know where we could get some of that polymer?" he asked Jackson. "Perhaps enough for a battering ram?"

"Don't even think about it," Megan said. She pushed past them and used the key to unlock the shed door. She flipped on a light switch, then groaned when nothing happened. "Hashemi . . ."

"Sorry. Coming," he said, rushing to the door. Once inside, he said, "Lights on, fifty percent. Heat, seventy percent."

The overhead floodlights and desk lamps slowly warmed to a dull yellow.

"What?" Jackson spun around. "What's happening?"

"Please don't get him started," Megan said, shedding her coat. "If he spent half as much time working on the

RhinoBot as he did on the MATE, we might actually have a functioning robot."

"And just what is a MATE?" Jackson asked.

Hashemi opened his book bag and pulled out a thick gray tablet. "Meet the MATE — the Most Awesome Tablet Ever, Version Four. It's the most technically astute and progressive tablet ever created."

"You're already on version four?" Megan asked. "Where are the first three prototypes? How much are you spending on that project?"

Hashemi nodded toward a stack of tablets on a bookshelf. "You can't put a price on technological progress."

"Yeah, but I can put a price on a brand-new china cabinet."

"Whatever happened to the phone you were working on?" Jackson asked.

"Why limit myself to five inches of screen on a smartphone when I can double that with a tablet?" He shrugged. "It's not like anyone actually calls me, anyway."

Jackson glanced at a dimly lit desk lamp sitting in the middle of the table. "And it controls the lights?"

"The lights, sound system, heat — it's all automated, run through the MATE, and calibrated to my voice. It can even start a computer remotely," Hashemi said. "I offered to authenticate Megan's voice as well, but she passed."

"I'm not carrying around a tablet to turn on a set of lights — not when an old-fashioned switch works just as well." She thumped his arm. "And how about you turn up the heat a bit more, Dungeon Master?"

Hashemi knew that he and Megan were just friends, but his skin buzzed, just a little, when her finger hit his arm. "Heat, eighty percent," he said.

"How long has all this been up and running?" Jackson asked. "A few weeks?"

Hashemi stopped smiling. "Two months."

"Oh." Jackson sat down at a worktable. "I guess it has been a while since I've popped in."

"Yes, it has," Hashemi said.

Jackson peeled off his coat. "Okay, let's just get to it. Are you guys going to tell me what's going on, or am I going to have to drag it out of you?"

Megan shifted her gaze. "I don't have any idea what you're talking about."

"Don't look to your right when you lie. It's a dead give-away," he said. "Let's try again. Where were you on Saturday night?"

"We went to the movies with some of the guys from Tech Club." Megan nudged Hashemi. "Right?"

Hashemi swallowed hard. He could already feel the sweat on his forehead. "Yes."

"That's interesting," Jackson said. "I emailed Keno before heading over here. According to him, you two never showed up at the theater."

"That *bruchon*," Megan muttered.

Jackson arched his eyebrow. "Klingon?"

"Romulan," Hashemi said. "It means 'traitor.' Technically it's noncanon, but if I ever get the Universal Translator working on the MATE —"

"Hash, you lost me at Romulan." Jackson leaned

forward. "Can I borrow the MATE? I need to show you guys something."

Hashemi reddened. "It's, um . . . well . . ."

"I know, I know." Jackson took the tablet. "It's in beta."

Megan sighed. "Just like the RhinoBot."

Jackson swiped the screen until he found the browser. He flipped open his notebook, mumbled something to himself, then typed in a web address. "Crowd around," he said. "You guys need to see this firsthand."

Hashemi and Megan circled the table to stand behind Jackson. A grainy video of the social studies wing flickered on the screen. Then a familiar face popped into view.

"Um, that's me," Hashemi said.

"And me," Megan added, a few seconds later.

Hashemi watched as he and Megan, both dressed in black, snuck into the first-floor girls' bathroom. A few seconds later, the video cut to Bradley, Charlie, and Jackson slipping into the boys' bathroom. They too were dressed in black.

"The entire video is about three minutes long, but trust me — there are clips of us sneaking into each bathroom at school as well as the security room." Jackson paused the video. "Then the water starts pouring out of the bathrooms. The video's a fake, obviously. But can we prove that?"

"Here, let me see the MATE," Megan said. She took the tablet and restarted the video. Once it was over, she turned to Hashemi. "What do you think?"

Hashemi slumped into a chair. "I wouldn't say 'impossible' . . . but it would most certainly be a challenge."

"That's saying it nicely." She placed the tablet on the table. "Here's the problem, Jackson. Since the base security video is of such poor quality, it's hard to tell the difference between the low-quality recording and errors from pasting our faces onto other people's bodies." She sighed. "I could eventually prove that it's a fake, but it would take a few months, along with some really high-end software."

"Meanwhile we'd miss out on the class trip to Cedar Point and the Battle of the Robots and any other activities that Dr. Kelsey wants to ban us from," Jackson said.

Hashemi looked toward his *Star Trek* shelf. "This is just like episode 141 of *Star Trek: Deep Space Nine*. 'In the Pale Moonlight.' Except, you know, we're not trying to start a war with an alien race."

"Yeah, I can see the resemblance," Jackson said. "So again, are you guys going to tell me where you were on Saturday or not? I'll be honest. I wasn't at the library. I was with Gaby. We were . . . reclaiming some funds from Eric Caan —"

"You mean Vizzini's Challenge?" Hashemi asked Jackson. "Gaby was telling us about that at lunch today."

Jackson rolled his eyes. Gaby was as bad as Charlie when it came to making up con names. "Forget that. It's not important. Just tell me where you were on Saturday night."

Hashemi settled into his seat. "We were —"

"Hashemi!" Megan yelled.

"We have to tell him," he continued. "He's Jackson Greene. He's going to figure it out anyway."

Jackson leaned against the edge of the table. "You guys were pulling a job with Charlie, weren't you?"

"No," Hashemi began. "Well, not exactly."

"We were just doing recon," Megan said. "We were at Riggins, casing the school. Me, Hash, Bradley — all of us." She shrugged. "Except you."

"Charlie told us about the Trophy Heist that you two planned a few years ago," Hashemi said. "He showed us your notes and everything."

"You mean the notes Charlie forged? In a notebook he stole from his sister?" Jackson glanced at his current notebook. It was almost full, and the cover was old and worn. "Riggins has made a lot of security upgrades since Charlie and I came up with that plan. There's no way I'd try to sneak into the school now. Charlie knows that."

Hashemi blinked. "But Charlie said —"

"Charlie lied," Jackson said. "But that's the least of our worries. Whoever's behind this knew you all would be at Riggins, and that I'd be at Eric Caan's house." He rubbed his jaw. "But who would want to frame us?"

"Keith?" Megan asked.

"Maybe. The person who made the video wants to meet tomorrow afternoon. Hopefully I'll find out more then."

"So that's it?" Hashemi asked. "All we can do is wait?"

Jackson nodded. "I'm open to suggestions, but until we know who we're dealing with, I'm all out of options."

Megan crossed her arms. "You sure seem relaxed for someone facing a two-week suspension."

"Rule Number Two of the Code of Conduct: Stay cool under pressure." Jackson picked up his coat. "Don't worry, guys. We're safe for the time being. Kelsey doesn't have the video. Without that, he can't take us to the Honor Board."

ON MY HONOR

"What do you mean, he's not bringing it to the Honor Board?"

Lincoln Miller gritted his teeth. It was way too early in the morning to be yelled at by Serena Bianchi. Although she was a seventh grader, Serena had skipped a grade in elementary school and was therefore the youngest member of the Honor Board. She was also a full foot shorter than Lincoln, but what she lacked in height and age she more than made up for in tenacity.

"The bylaws clearly state —"

"I know you don't like the result, but all I can tell you is what Dr. Kelsey told me yesterday afternoon," Lincoln said. "Without evidence —"

"He has Jackson's notebook and Charlie de la Cruz's bag." Her eyes, green with flecks of gray, cut into Lincoln. "What more evidence does he need?"

Lincoln looked around as the other Honor Board members quickly slipped out of the classroom. Even Mr.

Pritchard, their advisor, had retreated to his desk, suddenly engrossed in whatever was on his computer screen.

"Don't tell me they bought the school off like Keith Sinclair did."

Lincoln refocused on Serena. "No — and technically, we don't know that Mr. Sinclair's donation had anything to do with Dr. Kelsey reducing Keith's punishment."

"Based on Article —"

"You don't have to quote the Honor Code to me, Serena." He perched himself on the edge of the desk. "I don't necessarily agree with Dr. Kelsey, but he's right. Jackson's dad pointed it out to him. The bag and notebook are circumstantial evidence. He doesn't have enough proof that Charlie and Jackson flooded the school."

She shook her head, making her hoop earrings bounce against her neck. "But they don't have alibis."

"Jackson was at the public library. The staff at the front desk saw him enter and leave. He even reserved a study room. It's all on a log."

Serena began to pace in front of Lincoln. Lincoln was one of the most important students at Maplewood, she thought, at least in terms of his political power. She just didn't understand why he let himself be everyone's doormat. Dr. Kelsey's. Keith's. And especially Jackson Greene's. It was like he *enjoyed* being conned.

"You know the *Inf* — you know Jackson Greene could have easily snuck out of that library." She refused to use Jackson's silly nickname. "We can't let him get away with this. He breaks school rules. All. The. Time." She pushed her hair out of her face. "Don't you want to catch him? It'd be the greatest case ever for the Honor Board."

"That's not how it works," Lincoln said as he walked around Serena. "Our job isn't to catch thieves. We catch cheats."

"Aren't they the same?"

"Depends on the cheat." He paused at the door. "Look, we don't police the Honor Code. We rule on violations," he said. "And for what it's worth, Jackson Greene does way more good than bad for Maplewood."

Maybe it isn't our job to police the Honor Code, Serena thought as she walked to her desk to grab her books. *But that doesn't mean we can't do it.*

a PINCH OF THE TRUTH

As Serena Bianchi exited Mr. Pritchard's classroom, she nearly marched into Gabriela de la Cruz. Gaby swerved just in time to avoid a collision, mumbled, "Sorry," then continued around the corner. She burst into the *Maplewood Herald* student office, empty except for Charlie and Bradley.

Charlie looked up. "What's wrong?" he asked. The latest edition of the newspaper lay on the table in front of him.

Gaby grabbed her brother's arm skin, pinched, and twisted.

"Ouch! Gaby!" He pulled his arm free. "What are you doing?"

"I've been waiting to do that since yesterday!" She pinched his other arm. "The only reason I didn't yell at you before is because Jackson asked me to wait."

"Gaby! Stop!" Charlie broke away and slid backward. "Why are you —"

"I know about the notebook! I was saving that for his birthday!"

Bradley began packing up his books. "Maybe I should go. I can work on these graphics in the art room."

"No, you need to hear this," Gaby said. "Go on, tell him, Charlie. Tell him how you forged Jackson's handwriting in the notebook. How you tricked the crew into casing Riggins with you."

Bradley frowned. "I don't understand. . . ."

"He lied to you," Gaby said. "He stole from me, he forged Jackson's handwriting, and he *lied* to get you to go along with him." She planted her hands on her hips. "I'm just trying to figure out how the notebook and your messenger bag ended up in the bathroom this weekend. You'd better speak up now if you know more about the flooding than you're letting on."

Charlie held up his hands like he was giving up. "I promise, I didn't know anything about the prank until Monday morning," he said. "My bag and the notebook went missing right before winter break. I didn't worry too much about them — I had already shown the notebook to the guys, and they'd agreed to case Riggins with me based on it. I figured I'd left the stuff at Hashemi's shed or Bradley's house. But after Kelsey showed them to me yesterday, I started thinking that maybe they were stolen from my locker."

"Back up a second," Bradley said. "You forged Jackson's handwriting? Was the entire Trophy Heist a lie?"

"No. Not a lie." Charlie ran his fingers through his hair. "Okay, maybe the part where I copied Jackson's handwriting was a bit misleading, and maybe the plan didn't account for all of the school's new upgrades, but I would have eventually come up with a revised strategy for sneaking in. I just needed to do a little reconnaissance first."

"You can't be serious," Gaby said. "You know the Trophy Heist is suicide."

"I've snuck into Riggins before."

"Yeah, the Goat in a Blanket. I was there with you and Jackson, remember?" She shook her head. "But that was two years ago, before they installed all those electric key pads and motion sensors."

"I just can't believe you lied to us about the notebook," Bradley said.

"You're right — I shouldn't have done that, and I'm sorry," Charlie said. "But if we're being honest, you all would never have agreed to scope out the school if you knew it was my plan, not Jackson's."

Bradley paused to consider this.

"Stop trying to guilt him," Gaby said to her brother. "You're the one in the wrong here, not Bradley."

Charlie shrugged. "Why are we even talking about this? It all worked out okay. No one got hurt or caught or in trouble. Totally harmless."

"That's what you think." Gaby unlocked her phone and queued up the same video that Jackson had shown Hashemi and Megan the day before. She hit PLAY.

After a few seconds, Bradley asked, "Why are Megan and Hashemi sneaking into the girls' bathroom?" His eyes widened. "Wait — is that me?"

"Don't you remember? You and the others flooded the school on Saturday," Gaby said.

Charlie leaned closer to the screen. "That's impossible. We weren't anywhere near Maplewood on Saturday night."

"I know. But this video says otherwise." After it played through, Gaby returned her phone to her pocket. "You should talk to Jackson about this."

"No way," Charlie said, standing up. "I can handle it."

"Yeah, because you've done a brilliant job of managing *your* crew so far."

Bradley raised his hand, but after neither Charlie nor Gaby acknowledged him, he dropped it. "Maybe we should hear what Jackson has to say. Rule Number Eleven: Explore all options and possibilities before you make a decision."

Gaby frowned. "'Rule Number Eleven'?"

Bradley looked at Charlie, then Gaby. "Yeah, in . . . the de la Cruz Rules of Engagement."

Gaby rolled her eyes. "You really are a thief, aren't you?"

"Jackson's code had a few gaps," Charlie said. "And he didn't seem to be using it."

"Well, Jackson's involved now, whether you like it or not. He's being framed too. Whoever is behind this wants to meet with him this afternoon."

Charlie sank back in his seat. If Dr. Kelsey found out about that video, Charlie could wave his job as editor of the *Herald* good-bye. "Who would want to frame us?"

Bradley began counting off. "Keith Sinclair, Stewart Hogan, Victor Cho, maybe even the Honor Board. And of course, Dr. Kelsey," he said. "You have to admit, we made a lot of enemies during the Great Greene Heist."

"You don't have to keep calling it that. The Election Job is just fine," Charlie said. "What time is Jackson's meeting?" he asked. "I'll meet him after school and —"

"He said he was going alone," Gaby said. Her brother opened his mouth, but she cut him off. "Don't start. Believe me, I tried to convince Jackson to let someone go with him. But he was asked to go alone, so that's what he wants to do."

But it's my crew now, Charlie thought.

"I should go to the studio," Bradley said. "Mr. Jonas will be waiting on me."

Charlie punched Bradley on the shoulder and offered him a small smile. Bradley didn't smile back. "Hey, I *am* sorry for tricking you. And getting you into this mess," Charlie said. "I'll figure something out."

Gaby waited until Bradley left the room before turning toward her brother. "Proud of yourself?"

Charlie frowned at her. "Why are you even here? You aren't involved in this. This is between me, Jackson, and the rest of the crew."

"You're my brother, and Jackson's my . . ." Gaby tugged her ponytail as her face reddened. "I'm involved." She sat down across from him and glanced at the newspaper. Bradley had drawn the illustration for the lead article. "And it's kind of my fault that Jackson doesn't have an alibi on Saturday."

Charlie nodded. "I heard about Vizzini's Challenge. Nice job. How'd you sneak the faulty joysticks into Eric's house?"

"UPS. A Christmas gift from his dear aunt Maureen."

"And you guys actually taught yourselves how to play *Ultimate Fantasy IV* with broken joysticks?"

"What else were we supposed to do over the winter break?"

He shrugged. "I'm just surprised that you didn't tell me."

"I'm sorry. Jackson didn't want *anyone* to know he was pulling another con. He thought the crew might want in, and he wanted to keep the team as small as possible."

Of course they would want to be involved, Charlie thought. *He's Jackson Greene.*

"Anyway, you seemed pretty busy yourself. You know, with all the planning you were doing for the Trophy Heist." She crossed her arms. "Also, now would be a good time to apologize about the notebook."

He smiled. "I'm sorry. I'll replace it."

"I just don't understand why you'd want to pull a job like that. You don't even care about football."

"The only reason they stole the trophy is because we stole their mascot first."

"So what? Why risk breaking into a school over a trophy that no one's thought about for two years?"

Because Samuel Greene said it was impossible, he wanted to say. *Because Jackson's too scared to try it. Because nobody will think I'm Jackson's sidekick anymore if I pull it off. Because I'll be the best.*

Instead, he said, "I know Jackson didn't decide to help Lynne's brother on his own. You convinced him to do it, didn't you?"

Gaby tensed. "Yes, but I didn't trick him —"

"I know. I'm not accusing you of doing anything wrong. But tell me the truth. How did it feel, pulling the con with him?" He grinned as he picked up the newspaper and folded it in half. "I know you liked it."

Gaby rolled her eyes and turned toward the door. But she wasn't mad at Charlie.

She just didn't want him to see the smile on her face.

THIS IS **NOT** a TEST

"So what's with all the love for libraries?" Samuel Greene asked as he pulled up in front of the Shimmering Hills Library on Tuesday afternoon. After Jackson didn't respond, he put the car into park. "You okay? You've been quiet the entire trip."

Jackson nodded toward the radio. "Just trying to ignore that noise you keep playing every time we get into the car."

Samuel turned down the volume. He had been introduced to free jazz during his first semester at the University of Pennsylvania, and insisted on playing either Ornette Coleman or Pharaoh Sanders every chance he got during his semester break. "I know it's a little sophisticated —"

"Sophisticated? He's playing a plastic saxophone."

"Stop changing the subject. Something's up," he said. "Look, if you're too scared to kiss Gaby, you can always —"

"I'm not scared!" Jackson said. "I'm waiting for the right opportunity. Anyway, how old were you when you had your first kiss?"

Samuel actually looked a bit ashamed. "Oh, um . . . eleven. But I was a risk taker. Totally unlike you."

Jackson leaned against the headrest. He wished his brother had never told him about his stupid Rules of Romance. He knew he should ignore them, but every time he thought about Gaby — and how perfect he wanted that first kiss to be — his mind kept going back to Samuel's list. *Make sure it's private. Always carry a box of mints. Don't forget to close your eyes. Wait for the right opening.* "I'm not stressed out about that," he said. "I have an important meeting."

Samuel pointed at the notebook poking out of the top of Jackson's coat pocket. "I thought you had retired that thing."

"You never know when you'll need to write something down."

"Jackson —"

"Don't start." He glanced at a large box of watches in the backseat. "You don't have any business lecturing me about giving up cons."

"That's just a little side project. Something to keep me busy until I head back to Penn next week." Samuel pushed up his shirtsleeve, showing off his watch. "Want one? I'll give you a good deal."

"Um, no thanks."

"They look almost real. Just don't get them wet. The bands will turn your arm green."

"I hope they at least keep time correctly. I'll be finished in thirty minutes." Jackson opened the car door. "Or you could give me your cell phone and I could call you at home when I'm ready."

Samuel turned the music back up. Jackson resisted the urge to cover his ears. "Can't give you the phone," Samuel said. "It's not really mine."

"You stole it?"

"I repurposed it," he said. "The teaching assistant it belonged to only used it to stream pirated movies and text his girlfriends — including Carletta, my lab partner. I figured both she and the phone could do better."

"Don't be late," Jackson said before closing the door.

Samuel rolled down the window. "Have fun with all the studying, or whatever you're doing." His smile faded. "And Jackson — be safe."

Jackson's watch beeped six o'clock as he climbed the steps to the front door. It was almost too fitting, holding the meeting in the very library that he had snuck out of on Saturday evening. He spent a few seconds taking in the surroundings, trying to note anything or anyone that seemed out of place. It looked like a normal Tuesday.

Or maybe he was just rusty.

He worked his way to the second floor, then through the maze of shelves to the north end of the building. This section of the floor was filled with partitioned tables and small study rooms that patrons could reserve. The rooms usually smelled like cat urine and moldy bread — and the glass windows offered no real privacy — but they were soundproof.

Jackson's mouth dropped open as he peered into the

last room in the row. He slowly opened the door. "You two are behind this?" he asked.

Sitting smugly on the other side of the table were Rob Richards and Thom Jordan. Although they weren't related, most students thought they were brothers — they shared the same bland facial features, slight builds, and slimy dispositions.

Rob smirked. "What? Didn't think we had it in us?"

"You guys aren't exactly known for your intricate planning skills. And you could have saved us all a trip if you'd just talked to me after history." Jackson shut the door and sat down in the chair across from them. It felt too low, but there was no way for him to adjust it.

"Some things don't need to be discussed at school," Rob said before nudging Thom. "Let's get this over with." Thom rolled up his sleeve and glanced at the blue ink scrawled on his arm. Rob rolled his eyes. "You took notes?" he asked.

"Didn't want to forget anything." Thom read his arm to himself, his lips moving slightly, then looked up. "So first I'm supposed to thank you for showing up."

"You're not supposed to tell him what you're going to do. Just — oh, never mind." Rob yanked Thom's arm toward him and read the notes himself. "Thank you for coming, Jackson," he said, his voice monotone. "And thank you for showing up alone."

"Why don't you skip to the part where you tell me why I'm here? Is this revenge or blackmail? Or both?" Jackson played with the end of his tie, letting it flap against the table. "Maybe I'm mistaken, but I don't remember doing anything to you guys."

"You haven't," Thom said. "This is . . ." He paused dramatically. "Business." He smiled. "Like that? It wasn't even in the notes."

Rob gritted his teeth. "I should have come by myself," he mumbled. "Okay, here's the deal. The American history exam is next week. If we don't ace it — and I mean really ace it — Mrs. Clark will flunk us. We'll have to repeat the class in summer school."

"When you say 'ace it,' you mean you have to get an A?" Jackson asked.

"More like an A-plus," Rob replied. "A *high* A-plus."

Jackson pulled his notebook from his pocket. "So you want me to help you cheat during the test next week."

"No," Rob said. "We want you to steal the test so we can memorize the answers beforehand."

Jackson blinked a few times, waiting for them to laugh. They didn't. "Are you guys serious?"

They nodded.

"You're crazy. There's no way I'm doing that."

"Come on," Thom said, looking at his notes. "Are you telling me that the Infamous Jackson Greene is afraid?"

Jackson wanted to grab Thom's arm and look at it himself, if only to get the meeting over with. "Goading me isn't going to work. I'm out of the business."

"I'm not sure Eric Caan and the guys from Riggins would agree," Rob said.

Jackson shook his head. *No way Rob and Thom are*

smart enough to pull off something like this. Not by themselves. . . .

"Who's really behind this?" he asked. "Eric? Keith?"

"Wouldn't you like to know," Rob said, a wide smile spreading across his face.

"You know I can eventually prove that the video is a fake," Jackson said.

"Yes, but 'eventually' is a very long time," Rob said. "And do you really want to take that chance with Dr. Kelsey?" He leaned back in his chair. "So that's the offer. The exam for the video. Do we have a deal?"

Jackson was quiet for a few moments as he jotted down some notes. He knew Rob and Thom were staring at what he wrote, probably trying to decipher his code. They had a better shot at acing Mrs. Clark's exam.

"Do those fancy notes of yours say how much time I have to think this over?" he asked as he flipped his notebook shut.

"Twenty-four hours," Thom said, not even looking at his arm.

"It's the least we can do," Rob added. "Partner."

THE GANG'S ALL HERE

As Charlie de la Cruz biked to school early on Wednesday morning, he replayed his conversation with Jackson the night before over and over in his head. Jackson had described finding Rob and Thom in the library. He told him about Thom's arm, their failing grades, their pride in the blackmail scheme.

Then Jackson had *ordered* him to contact the rest of the crew and organize a meeting at Hashemi's shed. Like Charlie was his personal assistant. Like everyone should always obey the marvelous Jackson Greene.

So Charlie kept cool and did as he was instructed — except he moved the meeting from Hashemi's shed to the newsroom. There'd be no Jackson Greene swooping in to save the day, at least not this morning.

Charlie locked his bike in the otherwise empty rack, then entered the school. Most teachers hadn't arrived yet, which was why he chose such an early meeting time. The newsroom was down the hallway from Mrs. Clark's room, and he figured it was worth doing a little recon work after the meeting — just in case they really did decide to steal the exam.

He opened the door to the social studies wing, then paused as Mr. Hutton pushed an empty janitorial cart down the hallway toward him. Charlie stuck his hands in his pockets and folded his fingers around his laminated *Maplewood Herald* pass. The hallways were usually off-limits before school, but as a member of the newspaper staff, he was able to come and go to the newsroom as he pleased.

"Kind of early to be at school, Charlie," the custodian said.

"Editorial meeting. The news never sleeps, you know."

"Got a pass?" he asked.

Charlie flashed his badge. He hoped Mr. Hutton was finished with his work on this side of the building — Charlie hadn't bothered with creating badges for anyone else.

Apparently satisfied, the custodian started to walk away. "For what it's worth, I know you and Jackson are good kids," he said. "There's no way you two could be responsible for all this flooding."

Me and Jackson, Charlie thought as he entered the newsroom. *Of course.* It had been four months since the Election Job. Aside from the occasional video game, he and Jackson hardly hung out anymore. They certainly hadn't planned another job. So why did everyone still want to lump them together?

Bradley was the first to arrive. When Hashemi and Megan entered a few minutes after, they offered Charlie slight nods but continued past him to the table, both looking at something on Hashemi's new tablet.

Charlie began to close the door. "Before we start, I think I should apologize for —"

"Hey, guys," Jackson said, barging into the room. "Sorry I'm late."

"Jackson!" Bradley yelled, jumping out of his chair. He went to high-five him but missed, hitting Jackson's face instead. "Sorry," he mumbled.

"It's okay," Jackson said, blinking. "I never used my left eye that much anyway."

Bradley grinned. "I'm glad you're here. Had a change of heart?"

Jackson stopped wiping his eye. "What?"

"When Charlie texted us last night to set up the meeting, he told us that you were sitting this one out."

"There must have been a misunderstanding," Jackson said as he glanced at Charlie. "I just thought we were meeting at Hashemi's shed. Good thing I got up extra early."

Although Jackson was smiling, Charlie could see the anger in his eyes. But he wasn't going to let Jackson waltz back in and hijack his crew. "I have it under control," he whispered to Jackson.

"No, you don't." Jackson pushed past him and hoisted himself on top of the editor's desk at the front of the room. *Charlie's* desk. "Okay, I assume that Charlie's brought you all up to speed on my meeting with Rob and Thom."

"Yeah," Megan said. "Basically, if we don't steal the American history exam by next Friday, we're doomed."

"We've been in worse situations," Charlie said. He thought about sitting on the desk next to Jackson, but instead stood to his right. "We can find a way out of this. I have a —"

"Maybe we should go to Mrs. Clark," Hashemi said. The MATE's blue-tinted screen illuminated his face. "Pulling the Great Greene Heist was one thing, but stealing a test — especially one of *her* tests — is impossible."

Charlie's fingers tensed at the mention of the heist. "Nothing's impossible," he said.

"Maybe we should talk to Dr. Kelsey," Bradley chimed in. "He's not so mad about the heist anymore." He crinkled his nose. "Well, except when Keith's father calls. Or Gaby enters the office. Or —"

"Guys, I know you're worried," Jackson said. "I am too. This is really risky. But you know how Dr. Kelsey feels about us. He's been waiting four months to blame us for something, and now he has his chance."

"But the video is doctored," Bradley said. "We can prove it's a fake."

"Yes. Eventually," Megan said. "But not before Dr. Kelsey makes us withdraw from the Battle of the Robots."

"And not before he suspends us for two weeks and bans us from any school activities," Jackson added. "Knowing Kelsey, that's the tip of the iceberg."

"So you have a plan?" Hashemi asked.

Charlie watched his crew lean in and look up at Jackson.

Jackson grinned. "I'm working on it."

"Are we really going to steal the test?" Megan asked. "Like, for real?"

"Depends on how you define *we*."

"Maybe we can rig the scoring machine, like we did during the Great Greene Heist," Bradley said. "Maybe —"

Charlie slammed his fist on the desk. "Can you *please* stop calling it the Great Greene Heist?"

Hashemi cocked his head. "But . . . *you're* the one who started calling it that in the first place."

Charlie took a step backward. "Yeah . . . well . . . that was before —"

"Mrs. Clark grades her tests by hand," Jackson continued, speaking over him. "So no, we can't rig the machine like we did during the . . . *Election Job*. But like I said, I'm working on a plan."

"Well, I have a few ideas too," Charlie said, puffing his chest.

Jackson crossed his arms. "Does your plan involve you getting everyone caught on video?"

Charlie frowned. "What?"

"There are four cameras between the newsroom and the front doors," Jackson said. "And since I'm sure you've done your homework, you know that each camera has a built-in flash drive that can record up to twenty-four hours of video."

Charlie peeled off his scarf — the room had suddenly become unbearably hot. "But Hashemi and Megan said that the NVR wouldn't record without the hard drive. And since the cameras are Ethernet-powered, they have to be plugged into the NVR to work." He looked at Megan and Hashemi. "Right?"

Megan's face had become long and serious. "Correct. Without the hard drive, you can't manipulate video, watch all sixteen cameras in real time, or run any normal NVR operations. But that doesn't have anything to do with the cameras themselves."

"Think of it as a passive electrical system," Hashemi added. "It doesn't matter if the NVR is operational or not. As long as it's powered on and the cameras are plugged in, they will record to their flash drives."

Bradley slumped in his seat. "So what does all this mean? We're not in trouble for meeting in here, are we?"

"Technically, no students should be meeting without the faculty sponsor present, but no one ever really enforces that rule. That gets you and Charlie off the hook, since you're *Maplewood Herald* staff members," Jackson said. "Lucky for the rest of us, I've filled out the paperwork for us to join as well — backdated by two days." He pulled a stack of forms from his book bag. "All I need is your signatures."

Hashemi looked at his paper. "How did you figure out our school ID numbers?" he asked, squinting at the form. "*I* don't even have my number memorized."

"Let's not waste any time with frivolous details," Jackson said. "Just remember, if anyone asks, we were meeting about an exposé on the break-in. Not exactly a lie, if you think about it."

Megan scribbled her signature on her form and passed it back to Jackson. "Good going, Charlie. You want to leave a forged notebook lying around for someone to steal too? You're already on a roll."

"But I . . . How was I supposed to know —"

"Rule Number Twelve," Jackson said. "You've got to do your homework."

Everyone was quiet for a few seconds before Bradley raised his hand and said, "Rule Number Twelve. Is that from the Greene Code of Conduct or the de la Cruz Rules of Engagement?"

"The de la what?" Jackson asked.

If not for the chair in his path, Charlie would have taken another step back. "It's . . . It's nothing."

"So now what do we do?" Megan asked. Although the question was lobbed to the group, she was looking directly at Jackson.

Jackson pulled out his notebook. "Megan, I need you and Hash to figure out who forged the video. Whoever he or she is, they're good, which should limit the pool."

"For sure, no one at Maplewood did it," Megan said. "You're looking at the only two students here who could pull off a forgery that good, that quickly."

Hashemi blushed. "Thanks. I was —"

"Actually, I was talking about me and Bradley." She nudged Hashemi. "Photo and video manipulation isn't exactly your specialty. And no, designing app icons for the MATE doesn't count."

As Hash, Megan, and Bradley laughed, Jackson took them in. It really had been a while since he'd hung out with the crew. His friends. Hash and Megan sat close together — closer than they needed to. He wondered if they were more than just friends. Was it possible that Hash had the guts to kiss a girl, but he didn't?

Megan's laughter finally tapered off. "Anyway, I've been thinking — whoever did this has to be a whiz at graphic design *and* computers. There's only a handful of kids our age who can pull that off."

Hashemi looked at her. "You think it's Kayla Hall, don't you?"

She nodded. "She has the skills. She could probably recruit a few friends to help with the quick turnaround on the video manipulation." Then, quieter, she added, "And she has the motivation."

"Does she have a grudge against you two?" Jackson asked.

Hashemi tapped the MATE to wake it up. "Kayla's the president of the Robotics Club at Riggins. Megan beat her at the Battle of the Robots last year." He showed them a photo of a tank-shaped robot split in half, its red and white circuits spilled all over the floor. "The officials inspected her machine after receiving a complaint about her alleged used of contraband components. She was eventually barred from competing for two years."

"Were you the one who tipped off the officials?" Bradley asked Megan.

"Of course not," Megan said. "But I may have mentioned it in passing to the guys at Great Oaks Prep. They actually turned her in."

"So she's got a grudge. And she's got some free time on her hands. And she's a genius," Jackson said. "Anything else we should know?"

Megan picked at her thumbnail. "I may have sent her a nasty email or two, rubbing in the win."

"Well, I guess we know where you're starting first." Jackson made a mark in his notebook. "Bradley, can you try to figure out Mrs. Clark's testing routine? Maybe she turns in a copy of the scoring guide before the actual exam. Or maybe she uses student helpers. Anything would be helpful. And see if you can borrow a laptop and software from the graphic design guys. Without a bankroll, we're going to have to shake out our piggy banks and use whatever equipment we can get our hands on." He turned to Charlie. "And can you —"

"No thanks," Charlie said. "I'm sure you and the rest of Gang Greene can handle this without me." He grabbed his books and stormed out the door.

In the silence that followed, Jackson sighed and checked his watch. "Hash, can you text Gaby and ask her to talk to Charlie? She should be at school by now."

Hashemi typed a quick message on the MATE, then shoved it into his book bag. "You and Charlie are acting just like Kirk and Captain Decker in *Star Trek: The Motion Picture*," he said. "Kirk comes back to take command of the *Enterprise* and makes Decker the second in command."

"Is that from the new movies?" Bradley asked, grinning.

"You mean the series of movies where they give some cadet barely out of Starfleet command of the best ship in the galaxy?" Megan pretended to gag. "No way."

"I mean, it's the twenty-third century," Hashemi added. "You'd think they'd be smarter than that. If it had been Jean-Luc Picard or Kathryn Janeway, maybe I could see it. . . ."

"You had to get them riled up, didn't you?" Jackson said to Bradley. "And to be clear, I'm not trying to take anything over. But we've got less than ten days to figure a way out of this mess. We have to be organized and we have to be precise. Neither of those are Charlie's strengths."

"I'd follow you over Charlie any day," Megan said. "I hate liars."

"Megan, we're con artists. We're all liars." Jackson closed his notebook. "And to be fair, I've tricked both of you before too."

Megan paused. "Well, now that you mention it, yeah, you did. And that kind of sucked. But at least it was for a good reason — not to steal some stupid trophy." She turned to Hashemi. "And didn't Decker die at the end of that movie?"

Hashemi looked at the door. "Technically, he was only missing in action."

CIVIC **DUTY**

Serena sat on a bench in the empty atrium, eating an almond-and-flaxseed granola bar and sipping from a container of organic milk. She preferred getting to school early. Once the bell rang, the other students were always in her way, forcing her to dodge their overstuffed book bags and sharp, scaly elbows. They acted like they owned the hallways, just because they were bigger than her.

Serena's sister, Valencia, was a senior at Shimmering Hills High. She dropped Serena off every morning, even though it made Valencia almost an hour early herself. Valencia used to complain, but now she spent the extra time in the orchestra room practicing her cello. *Becoming even more perfect*, Serena thought.

Then Charlie de la Cruz burst through the social studies hall double doors. His face was red, and his hands were balled into fists. He didn't seem to notice Serena as he stomped across the atrium toward the vending machines.

Seconds later, Gaby slipped into the atrium, her phone tight in her hand. She sped up as Charlie started to move away from her. "Charlie, just hold on for a second," she called after him. "Carlito . . ."

Charlie stopped. Serena couldn't see his face, but by the way he was standing — arms crossed, back stiff — she could tell he was upset. Gaby came over and placed her hand on his shoulder.

Then Gaby glanced to her left and noticed Serena. She offered Serena a half wave before taking her brother's arm and leading him outside.

Serena slurped the last of her milk. It wasn't odd seeing Charlie at school this early. He often arrived before the other students to work on the newspaper. Gaby often came early as well, usually for some Student Council function. But that tension between them — *that* was interesting.

A few minutes later, Bradley Boardman, a sixth grader and another member of the news staff, exited the social studies hallway. Then Jackson Greene, Hashemi Larijani, and Megan Feldman entered the atrium, and Serena stopped chewing her granola bar. Unless those three had joined the *Herald* in the past couple of days, Serena was sure they had no business being in that hallway.

Like Bradley, they didn't notice her as they exited the atrium. They were talking too low for her to hear them, but that didn't matter. She'd seen everything she needed to see.

Gang Greene was back in action.

SEALING THE DEAL

Jackson tried to pay attention during class, but instead of listening to Mrs. Clark's soliloquy on the genius of Alexander Hamilton, he kept staring at the back of Rob Richards's head. Who were Rob and Thom working with? Keith Sinclair? After a weeklong suspension, he had stayed out of trouble. He even worked as an office helper, doing Kelsey's grunt work in order to remain on the principal's good side.

No, Keith didn't make sense. But if not him, who? Victor Cho? Stewart Hogan? Or was it someone else — someone Jackson hadn't even considered yet?

After the bell rang, Rob sprang from his seat and sped toward Jackson. Thom followed a few steps behind.

"So what did you decide?" Rob asked.

Jackson glanced toward the front of the room. A small group of students waited in line to talk to Mrs. Clark. "Not here," he said. "Meet me in the hallway. By the stairs."

Once Rob and Thom left, Jackson caught Hashemi's eye and quickly shook his head. He wanted to keep Hash and the others away from Rob and Thom as much as possible.

Jackson moved toward the door, slowing as he approached Mrs. Clark's file cabinet. With all its rust, scuffs, and dents, it looked at least as old as the school. He pretended to look through one of the room's three windows. Once he was sure the teacher wasn't watching, he gently pressed the latch and tugged on the handle to the top drawer.

Locked. Not that he expected anything else.

He stepped out of the room. Rob and Thom stood halfway down the hallway . . . with *Charlie*. Talking. While surrounded by teachers and other students.

As Jackson rushed toward them, he saw Keith Sinclair and Victor Cho coming his way. Neither Victor nor Keith glanced at Rob, Thom, and Charlie as they passed. Everything seemed like business as usual.

Jackson barged in between Charlie and Rob. "What are you guys doing?" he whispered.

"Charlie was just filling us in," Rob said. "So you're in?"

Jackson glared at Charlie, who seemed to shrink back a little. Then Jackson motioned for them to huddle around one of the industrial-sized recycling bins that the Environmental Action Team had placed around the school. "Open your textbook," he said to Rob. "Prop it up and pretend you're asking me a question."

Rob paused. "But I don't have my book."

Jackson rolled his eyes. No wonder the boys were about to flunk. He opened his book and placed it on top of the bin. Rob, Thom, and Charlie crowded around him. "Yeah, we're in," Jackson whispered, pointing to a random word on the page. "We'll get you the test. But you have to give us the video first."

"No way," Rob said. "We'll hand it over once you've given us the test. But not before."

Jackson flipped a page in the book. He hadn't expected the boys to give up the video, but he had to ask. "Okay. I'll be in touch next week. After we get the test."

"Unh-unh," Rob said. "Thom and I should be part of your crew."

"Absolutely not," Jackson and Charlie said together. Jackson glared at him again, but this time, Charlie didn't back down. "I don't need you two bumbling around, messing things up," Charlie said. "Me and my guys will handle it."

Jackson wished he had a piece of duct tape to put over Charlie's mouth. "What Charlie means is that it'll be safer and faster if we go in and get it," he said. "And less risk to you guys."

"That's not an option," Rob replied. "We've been . . . encouraged to tag along, to make sure you actually get the test." He pulled out his phone. "So when is the crew meeting again?"

"In the newsroom, like this morning?" Thom added, looking at Charlie.

Jackson quickly flipped another page, almost ripping

it out of the book. "No. At Hashemi's shed," he said. "We'll send you the address."

Rob leaned against the recycling bin. "Don't try to pull anything on us, Jackson. We're way ahead of you."

Jackson slammed the book shut and stuffed it in his bag. "Like I said, we'll send you the address." He grabbed Charlie's arm and began pulling him away. "Let's go."

Charlie shook Jackson off but still followed him down the hallway. Rob and Thom walked away in the other direction.

And Serena Bianchi stood in the doorway of Mr. Hunt's class, taking it all in.

THE SOUNDING BOARD

Gaby slipped her book bag off her shoulders and began unzipping it as she sped down the hallway. She had spent longer than she had planned talking with the Mathlete team and was now close to being late to her own Student Council meeting. But if her school-wide Coins Against Cancer project was going to be a success, she knew she had to reach out to every organization for their support, including the six Mathletes.

She rounded the corner, then slowed down. Jackson was leaning against her locker.

"Hey, Gaby," he said, moving out of her way. "I know you've got your Student Council meeting today —"

"I have time." She looked at her watch. "Well, I have five minutes." She swapped a few books into her bag, then closed her locker. "Is this about Charlie?"

"No, but thanks for trying to talk to him," he said as they walked back down the hallway. "Not that I think it'll do any good. He's so stubborn. . . ."

"Try to see where he's coming from," she said. "He's been running that crew for months. And now here you come, and just like that, you're back in charge."

"I don't want to lead the crew," Jackson said.

"Yeah, right."

"Really, I don't," he said. "It's just . . . Hash, Megan, Bradley, even Charlie — they're all my friends. I don't want them to get hurt or in trouble. And if they're going to run jobs, they need a leader who knows what he's doing. Who sees all the angles. Charlie's great at logistics and information gathering, but he's not a big-picture guy."

"So why don't you just tell him that?"

"I would if I thought he wouldn't get mad. You know how Charlie is. Anyway, I figure he and I will have plenty of time to sort things out after this is over." Jackson opened the hallway door for Gaby and let her enter the atrium before him. "But even I have to admit that we're in some real trouble. There are just too many holes."

Gaby slowed down to let two homeroom representatives pass by, then asked, "You mean like not knowing who Rob and Thom's mastermind is?"

"Mastermind? So we're giving him a title now?"

"Or *her*," Gaby said.

Jackson loosened his tie and smiled apologetically. "You're right. Sorry about that. I should know better than to jump to conclusions." He sighed. "But yeah, it's pretty hard to plan a job when you don't even know who you're trying to con. And think about it — why does . . . *the mastermind* need *us* to steal the test from Mrs. Clark's room? If Rob and Thom can break into the security room to steal the hard drive from the NVR, you'd think they could break into her classroom."

"Maybe they don't know how to pick the lock on her file cabinet."

"But even then, why steal the hard drive?" Jackson opened his notebook. "Why not take the entire NVR?"

"Maybe it was too big. A hard drive would be a lot easier to carry and hide." Gaby stopped a few feet from the auditorium. "You should really talk to Charlie. He might have some ideas. You guys are always better together."

Jackson took his pencil and crossed out a line in his notebook. "There's not much to talk about. Plain and simple, we're in over our heads. We should walk away."

Gaby waited for a few seconds for him to continue, but he just looked at his notebook and shook his head. Finally, she whispered, "But you're not going to walk away, are you? You're going to steal the exam."

He closed his notebook. "Maybe. But first we're going to do a little recon and see if we can't learn more about the mastermind."

"How?"

Jackson smiled. "It may involve a bit of breaking and entering on school property. . . ."

Gaby glanced at the auditorium, then back at Jackson. "You know I can't —"

"I know," he said. "You're Student Council president. You have other responsibilities."

"But if I could —"

"Then you'd be right there."

"I'll find another way to pitch in," she said. "I can talk to Dr. Kelsey . . . see if he knows anything more. Or maybe I can make some calls, see if any of the club presidents have heard anything. Or I could —"

"Gaby, it's okay," he said. He began to walk away. "And don't worry — I'll keep an eye on Charlie to make sure he doesn't get into too much trouble."

Gaby lingered by the door, watching Jackson disappear down the hallway. *But if you're looking after Charlie,* she thought, *who's going to look after you?*

OUTSOURCING

"Let me do all the talking," Megan said as she and Hashemi rounded the corner to Briscoe Lane. According to the MATE, it was only supposed to be a quick 7.28-minute stroll from the bus stop to Kayla's house. They had finally found the right street after twenty minutes of walking, when Megan forced Hashemi to turn off the tablet and ask for directions.

"So what exactly are you going to say?" Hashemi asked. "You can't just knock on her door and accuse her of forging the video."

"Why not?" Megan asked. "What's wrong with being direct?"

"What if we're wrong?"

"You saw her message. She was practically bragging through the screen."

Megan had emailed Kayla earlier that day, asking if they could drop by to discuss a joint social between the Maplewood Tech Club and the Riggins Robotics Club. The other girl had replied:

Let's meet today. I'll be at home, working on a small video project for a friend. Nothing major — just some light Photoshopping. Adding water effects can be such a bore.

P.S. If you can't meet in person, we can always video chat. I hear you guys are really comfortable on camera.

Kayla's house sat halfway up the block, with skeletons of birch trees overhanging the two-story structure. Megan opened the wrought-iron gate, crossed the large yard, and climbed the steps. But before she or Hashemi could ring the buzzer, the door opened.

Kayla held up a small tablet. "Saw you guys walking up. You can never have too much security."

Megan hated to admit it, but there were a number of similarities between her and Kayla Hall. She had always thought of herself as the rare techno-geek who didn't sacrifice fashion for science, and Kayla seemed the same way. Kayla's braids were pulled back into a bun without a stray strand in sight. Her glasses — dark blue frames with a slight tint — were trendy enough to be fashionable and comfortable-looking enough to be practical.

"Thanks for having us over." Megan reached out her hand, and Kayla shook it. It was a cold grip. Cold and strong.

"Let's talk in my room," Kayla said. As they passed the kitchen, she waved her hand at the table. "Cookies? Mom just baked them."

Megan shook her head, then slapped Hashemi's arm when he reached for the platter. "We're not hungry," she said.

Kayla shrugged, picked up a cookie, and continued to her bedroom.

Actually, "bedroom" wasn't quite the right word. It was more of a hybrid study and computer lab, with a bed and dresser shoved in the corner like an afterthought. An L-shaped desk hugged the two longest walls, and the number of monitors, laptops, and circuits that topped it could rival the electronics in Hashemi's shed. Bookshelves lined another wall and held both more computer equipment and models of *Battlestar Galactica* ships. Megan couldn't tell for sure, but it looked like Kayla owned both the rebooted and retro versions of the Colonial Viper.

"Like it?" Kayla asked.

Megan realized that she'd been staring at the retro Viper. "Sure. It's okay."

"I made it myself," Kayla continued. "It's to scale and everything."

"Cool," Hashemi said as he stepped closer to the models. "I thought about trying to build the Viper, but I didn't have room for both it and the *Enterprise* 1701-D in my closet."

"Well, I'd think not," Kayla said. "The *Enterprise* is a Galaxy-class starship, you know."

"Exactly! I thought about trying to build it at a smaller scale, but I —"

"Maybe we should get down to business," Megan said. This was war. They should not be fraternizing with the enemy.

"Fair enough," Kayla said. She sat down at her desk, then pointed to a small couch. Once Megan and Hashemi had settled into their seats, she said, "You're here because of the doctored security video, right?"

"Told you," Megan murmured to Hashemi.

"So you're admitting to it?" Hashemi asked. "You actually framed us?"

"Um, duh. Didn't you read the email?" Kayla looked at Megan. "This is your ace hardware guy? Thought he'd be a little quicker on the uptake."

Megan crossed her arms. "Slow and steady wins the race." It was okay for her and the rest of Gang Greene to make fun of Hashemi, but not Kayla.

"But why?" Hashemi leaned forward and wiped his hands on his khakis. "What did we do to you?"

"Ask Megan."

"What? Is this about you cheating at the Battle of the Robots last year?" Megan asked.

"It wasn't cheating. I was just using an advanced processor."

"Which was against the rules," Megan said. "And it's not my fault you got caught. I didn't turn you in."

"No, you just gossiped about it, then rubbed it in," Kayla said. She swiped at her tablet, cleared her throat, then said, "Let me see if this email rings a bell. 'Congratulations! I know you got disqualified, but at least your robot lasted two minutes in the ring. Think about how quickly you would have lost if you *hadn't* cheated.'"

Megan shrugged. "I said, 'Congratulations.'"

"Or how about this: 'Better luck next year — oh, I mean in two years.'"

"You're taking it out of context," Megan said. "You have to read between the lines."

"You really sent those emails to her?" Hashemi asked.

"Just friendly banter between two rivals," she replied. "But gossiping and trash talk is one thing," she said to Kayla. "You're actually framing us. Where's the ethics in that?"

"Ethics don't pay for motherboards," Kayla said. "My parents cut me off. Said I spent too much time and money on computers. Lucky for me, I received an offer from an alternate source of financing."

"Can you at least tell us who's behind this?" Hashemi asked. "Is it Rob and Thom?"

"No, they're just middlemen. Pawns. And before you even start — I'm not saying anything more about my contact." She turned toward one of her three oversized monitors and logged onto her computer. "So I *could* play you the doctored video again. It's right here on my desktop and it looks great in high-def. But if you ask nicely, I'll actually show you *how* I doctored the video."

Hashemi looked at Megan. Her mouth was in full frown mode, and her eyebrows were bunched and angry. He figured it might be best if he spoke for both of them. "Yes, we would like to see that."

Kayla glanced over her shoulder. "Megan?"

The lines deepened in Megan's face, but she gave a quick nod. "Yes, please," she mumbled.

Grinning, Kayla shifted a few boxes from her desk, exposing a small black box.

"You have a KRX Supreme security system too?" Hashemi asked.

"Yep, just like the one from your school." She spun the machine, popped out the hard drive, then inserted a new one. "Those KRX guys really know their hardware, but boy, do they make you pay for it."

Hashemi nodded. In addition to the sixteen cameras, the network video recorder, and the proprietary eight-terabyte hybrid hard drive, the KRX Supreme security package also came with specially tailored software that made it virtually impossible to crack. The only thing more inflated than its specs was its cost.

Kayla attached a cable from the NVR to her massive desktop computer, waited a few seconds for the security system log-in to pop onto the screen, then hunched over the keyboard. "I've been warned not to let you guys get too close to this — that you all have a habit of taking things that don't belong to you." She leaned back after a few keyboard clicks. The center monitor was broken into sixteen quadrants. "This is the hard drive from the NVR from Maplewood. I took the footage from it to create the video this weekend."

"Wait a minute." Hashemi straightened his glasses. "You modified that video by yourself? Over the weekend?"

Before Kayla could respond, Megan said, "Of course she didn't. No one can doctor a video that quickly. Not alone. Not even her."

Kayla grinned again — it was clear she was enjoying this. "Let me show you something." She began rewinding one of the videos. "The great thing about the NVR hard drive is that it holds up to three months of recorded footage," she said. "Plenty of images of you all to pick from."

"I don't care how much video you had," Megan said. "There's no way you could have pulled this off. Not without a green screen. It's . . ." She trailed off as Kayla paused the video, freezing on an image of Hashemi and Megan walking down a hallway . . . painted blue.

"It's a good thing your school colors are blue and red." Kayla restarted the video. "Not as ideal as a green screen for a background, but it works well enough." She turned toward them. "And it only took a few hours to make the video, not a full weekend, thank you very much."

Hashemi watched as he and Megan disappeared off camera. As good as Megan and Bradley were with video manipulation, there was no way they could create a video like that.

"Just in case you get any ideas about breaking into my room to steal the video, there are sixteen cameras monitoring my house. And by tomorrow night, I will have delivered the final video, wiped the hard drives clean, and purged all traces of the video from my desktop. I probably should have done all that after getting your email, but you can't blame me for showing off." She winked. "Just friendly banter between two rivals."

Megan shook her head. "I can't believe you're doing this. You're a . . . a . . ."

"An opportunist," Kayla said. "Look, even the best forgeries can be proven as fakes. I mean, you won't be able to trace it back to me — I'm not that careless — but you'll be able to clear your names." She logged off the machine. "Worst case, if you don't do what they want, they're going to give the video to the principal at the end of next week, right? Then it might take three or four months, but even Megan can eventually prove that the video's fake."

"But the Battle of the Robots is in three weeks," Hashemi said.

Kayla shrugged. "What's life without a few obstacles?"

Neither Hashemi nor Megan spoke as Kayla let them out. It wasn't until they were almost at the bus stop that he cleared his throat and said, "Tell me the truth. How bad is it?"

Megan shook her head. "Even if I worked twenty-four-seven and had the best equipment in the world, I couldn't prove that the video is a fake in three weeks." She stopped. "Do you think Jackson could sneak into her house and swipe the hard drives from the NVR or her desktop? We both know that it's impossible to erase everything from a drive. I'm sure I could find traces of the video if I poked around long enough."

"I don't know. Breaking into her house could get him into some serious trouble —"

"But sneaking into a school and stealing a test is *totally* harmless." She shoved her hands into her pockets. "Maybe I could hack her system remotely."

"Megan, there's no way you can —" He stopped once he noticed the look on her face. "I mean, you're an excellent hacker. The best, even. But Kayla's very good as well. Think how hard it would be to hack *your* computer system. Hers would be just as difficult."

She sighed. "At least we know her computer password has ten characters and the NVR password has twelve."

"What were you doing, counting clicks?"

"Of course," Megan said. "Weren't you?"

HONESTY IS THE BEST POLICY

Jackson slipped on his coat as he entered the living room. His parents sat on the couch, watching television. "I know it's getting late, but can I run over to the de la Cruzes'?" Jackson said. "I need to drop something off."

His father didn't turn away from the TV. "Have fun."

"Not so fast," Jackson's mother said. "There's something your father and I want to discuss with you."

"Now?" Donald Greene mumbled. "They're about to go into Final Jeopardy."

"Donald . . ."

His father sighed, then muted the television. "Sit down, Jackson."

Jackson slowly moved to the recliner. His mother stared intently at him, while his father's gaze remained on the television screen, his lips moving as he read the final clue.

"Oh, for crying out loud." Miranda Greene snatched the remote from her husband and paused the television. "The answer is 'Video Killed the Radio Star.'"

His father scratched his chin. "You could have at least said it in the form of a question."

Jackson clicked a few buttons on his new digital watch, a Christmas gift from his grandparents. He hadn't expected to get much use out of it, but when December came and went without a cell phone, he decided to start wearing it. "Can this wait until I get back? I'll just be gone for a few minutes."

"We'll let you go in a second," his father said. "First, your mother and I want to talk about the prank at the school."

"Like I said, I didn't do it."

"We're not saying that you did," his father said. "But we have questions. How do you explain the notebook?"

"And Charlie's messenger bag?" his mother chimed in.

"I don't know," Jackson said. "But I promise, it wasn't me. Or Charlie."

"So you're saying that you were in the library the entire time?" his father asked.

Jackson closed his eyes and took a deep breath. He wanted to make sure his voice was sure and steady. It was one thing to keep pieces of the truth from his parents; it was another to outright lie to them. "I didn't sneak into the school on Saturday afternoon," he said. "I just started hanging out with Gaby again. There's no way she'd let me do something so stupid."

Donald Greene relaxed in his chair. "Gaby *is* pretty levelheaded," he admitted. "You could do worse for a girlfriend."

Jackson stiffened. "She's not my —"

"I know, I know," he said, holding up his hands. "Miranda, were we that cute when we first met?"

"When we first met, you were hitting on my roommate."

"No, I was *conning* your roommate into giving me the phone number to her dorm room. *Your* dorm room." He winked. "It worked, didn't it?"

"Yes. Much to the disappointment of my parents." Miranda Greene turned back to her son. "You and Charlie know everything that happens at that school. If you have any idea who pulled the prank, you should tell Dr. Kelsey."

Jackson shook his head. "Rule Number Four: Never rat."

Miranda Greene crossed her arms and eyed her husband.

"Jackson, you're not helping matters," Donald Greene said. "And to be honest, the Code of Conduct doesn't always apply — especially in middle school." He shifted in his seat. "If you know who did it, you should say something. It might go a long way to gaining Dr. Kelsey's trust."

"Dr. Kelsey will never treat me like a normal student," Jackson said. "Samuel ruined that before I even got to Maplewood."

His mother slowly nodded. "He never did get over your brother filling his office with baby crickets."

"Allegedly," Jackson and his father said together. Jackson checked the time again. "Mom, Dad . . . it's getting late."

"You know, for a girl who's not your girlfriend, you sure have been spending a lot of time at Gaby's house," his father said. "Of course, not when her father's there. . . ."

"Are you still afraid of Hector de la Cruz?" His mother laughed. "He's just giving you a hard time."

"Trust me, fathers don't like anyone dating their daughters. It took months for your granddad to warm up to me."

"Try years," Miranda Greene said. "But Hector really does like you, Jackson."

"First of all, I'm not afraid of Gaby's dad," Jackson said. "Second, I don't *just* spend time with Gaby. I was with Hash and the guys this morning. And tomorrow we're all hanging at the shed."

"Wait," Jackson's mother said. "Who exactly is 'Hash and the guys'?"

Jackson rubbed the back of his neck. "Hash and Megan. And Bradley. And Charlie. And Gaby."

She sat up. "What are you all up to?"

"Nothing."

She turned to Jackson's father. "Don't you have anything to say about this?"

He took the remote from his wife and resumed the show. "As Dad used to say, the crew that plays together stays together." Then he smiled as the first contestant gave the correct answer. "How about that. You were right."

"I'm always right," Miranda Greene said. She nodded toward the door. "Don't be over there too long, Jackson. It's almost time for dinner."

Jackson began fastening his coat. "Mom, don't worry about me and the guys. We're just getting ready for Mrs. Clark's exam." He flashed her the infamous Greene smile. "Honest."

SECOND PLACE

Charlie reread the note he had found taped to his bike handlebars that morning. He had recognized Jackson's handwriting, but the message made no sense. He also had no idea how Jackson had snuck into their garage.

Although he wanted to ignore the note, he did as it instructed. He was still mad at Jackson for, well . . . for being right about everything, but he also knew that much of this was his fault. He shouldn't have talked to Rob and Thom at school. He shouldn't have moved the meeting from the shed to the newsroom.

And if he was really being honest with himself, he should never have tried to run his own crew.

Once at school, he hugged the line of trees adjacent to the parking lot, staying as far away from the building as he could. He stopped at the cedar with the red ribbon tied around its trunk. After leaning his bike against the tree, he crouched at the edge of the parking lot and glanced at the new digital watch he'd found strapped to his bike along with the note. At exactly 7:32:15, he ran full throttle across the parking lot, aiming himself at a large overhead light pole with another red ribbon around it. He stopped at the pole, almost skidding into it, and dropped into a crouch again. He checked his time — eleven seconds. Then, forty-five seconds later, he took off again, this time toward the school garden. He slowed down just enough that he didn't ram into the fence, then quickly scrambled over the top railing. He landed in a heap, then glanced at the watch again. "Fourteen seconds," he mumbled.

"Sixteen."

Charlie looked up as Jackson rounded the corner of the wooden toolshed. He held a thermos in each hand, and a stopwatch hung around his neck.

"I bet Gaby could have done it in eight," Jackson said as he sat down with his back against the shed.

Charlie sat down across from him. "Coffee?"

"Tea. Earl Grey. It's better for your pores." Jackson offered him a thermos. "And don't get too attached to my watch."

Charlie drank, then stuck out his tongue. He never understood how Jackson could stomach this stuff. It was way too hot and way too bitter.

Jackson started to speak but stopped as a car pulled into the school lot. He waited until it had passed. "Okay. I'm only going to say this once. You pull anything like you did yesterday again, and you're out."

Charlie blinked. *But it's my crew*, he wanted to say.

"First off, you had no business moving the meeting," Jackson said. "I get it — you're mad at me for whatever reason — but you can't let personal feelings cloud your judgment. It makes you sloppy and reckless. I've already heard from a few sources that Kelsey knows we were all in the newsroom together." Jackson took a sip of tea. "And what in the world were you thinking, talking to Rob and Thom? Thanks to you, we've got two amateurs tagging along."

"But I didn't tell them about the meeting in the newsroom."

"You'll forgive me if I find that hard to believe," he said. "Maybe you didn't tell them. Maybe they followed you that morning. Or maybe they heard from Dr. Kelsey. Or maybe someone else saw us and squealed."

Charlie started to speak but decided against it. Now didn't seem like the time to tell Jackson about seeing Serena Bianchi in the atrium yesterday morning, and again when they were talking to Rob and Thom.

"All I know is, if you'd kept the meeting at Hashemi's shed like we planned, and more importantly, if you'd kept your mouth shut, we wouldn't be in this mess."

Charlie switched the thermos from one hand to the other. "Rob and Thom would have eventually figured out that we were meeting somewhere and would have forced us to include them," he mumbled, more to the ground than to Jackson.

"Yes." Jackson drank from his thermos again. "But not before I'd gotten everyone together to explain the plan."

Charlie perked up. "You have a plan?"

Jackson pulled out his notebook. "It's a bit rough around the edges, but I think it'll work."

Charlie leaned over and glanced at the notebook,

though he hadn't yet figured out how to read Jackson's shorthand. "Want to talk it through? Maybe I can help."

Jackson flipped through the pages. "I already ran it by Hash."

"Oh. I see." Charlie felt like he'd been pelted with a snowball. "So the only reason you made me go through all that running and jumping and stuff was just to prove that you're in charge?"

"No. That's *your* part of the plan. . . . But only if you want to do it." His gaze met Charlie's again. "It's the most complicated task."

Charlie understood what Jackson was saying. "Complicated" meant that it posed the biggest risk of getting caught. "I'll do it."

"Are you sure? I don't want to force you into —"

"You're not forcing me to do anything," he said. "I'm volunteering."

"Fair enough," Jackson said. "So, like I mentioned yesterday, the cameras are still recording."

Charlie ducked. "Like right now?"

"Don't worry — Megan ran a few calculations. There's only one camera close enough to record us out here, and as it's currently positioned, its aim is too shallow to reach the garden."

So Megan knew more than he did too. "Where do I come in?" Charlie asked.

"With the cameras still recording, we can't just walk in and steal the test," Jackson said. "But maybe we can outrun them."

SERENA ON THE CASE

Serena readjusted her hat, pulling it lower over her ears, then jogged in place. A few students passed, but she refused to move from her spot on the sidewalk. She was there first, she figured. Let *them* be the ones to walk around *her*.

She hated giving up her usual atrium bench, but she wanted to catch Lincoln as soon as possible that morning. She also wanted to talk to him outside, away from all the other students. Jackson Greene had a lot of friends — friends who were probably more than happy to eavesdrop on his behalf.

Finally, the Millers' burgundy minivan pulled into the parking lot. Serena marched forward and met Lincoln as soon as he stepped onto the sidewalk.

"Um . . . Good morning?" he mumbled.

"He's up to something," she said. "I know it."

Lincoln waved to his mother as she drove off, then turned back to Serena. "You mean Jackson?"

"Who else? I saw him and Charlie talking in the garden when I got to school this morning. Yesterday morning, he and his entire team met up in the newsroom."

"Jackson's not a member of the newspaper staff."

"He is now," Serena said. "Jackson, Megan, Hashemi — they all joined. I checked myself."

"Well, that's not against the rules —"

"Then later on Wednesday, I saw Jackson and Charlie plotting something with Rob Richards and Thom Jordan. I couldn't hear them, but with the way they were talking — all quiet and secretive — I could tell they were up to something devious." She paused, noticing the deep frown on Lincoln's face. "Okay, maybe not devious. But still, they're up to something."

"Is that all you have?" Lincoln asked.

She blew out a long stream of air. "I told Dr. Kelsey and Mr. James about Jackson and his friends. Mr. James reviewed the video footage and confirmed that they were meeting in the newsroom. They think —"

"Wait. The security system still works?"

Serena nodded. "Even though the NVR hard drive was stolen, the cameras can still record."

Lincoln scratched his head. "How?"

"I don't know. I didn't ask for details." She really wished Lincoln would stop asking questions and let her finish. "Apparently, because of the way the system works, they can't use the NVR to sort through the recorded footage — something about it having to be saved on the NVR hard drive, not the cameras." She took a deep breath.

"What's important is that, in order to monitor Jackson, they need to review all the video from each camera every day before it records over itself. So I volunteered to pitch in."

"You agreed to look at twenty-four hours of security camera videos? For all sixteen cameras? Every day?"

"I've got time in the morning and during study hall. And at lunch. And after school."

Lincoln started toward the building. Serena fell into step beside him. "Of course, I can't stop you from helping out," he said, "but that's a lot of video to review."

Serena had been doing the math herself. Even if she fast-forwarded through each video at its highest speed, it would take an hour to go through each camera.

"Mr. James said that it's supposed to go a lot faster with a working NVR," she said. "Any idea when they're replacing the hard drive?"

"Next year. It seems that those hard drives are crazy expensive." Lincoln stopped at the front doors. "Are you really sure Jackson Greene flooded the school?"

"Who else is smart enough to pull off a prank like that?"

"But that's the thing," Lincoln said. "Whoever pulled that prank left evidence. Jackson would never have done that."

"Maybe it wasn't Jackson who made the mistake. Maybe it was Charlie. Or Bradley. Or . . ."

She trailed off as she saw Charlie de la Cruz biking toward the school. He slowed as he seemed to notice them. Then he turned and headed to another bike rack.

"He's avoiding us," Serena said.

"Or maybe he just wants to lock his bike up somewhere else." Lincoln pressed his fingers against his temples. "Okay, I'll talk to Gaby. Maybe there's some extra money in the Student Council budget that can go toward a new hard drive."

Serena huffed. "Yeah, good luck with that."

"She's fair."

"She's also got googly eyes for Jackson Greene. And she's Charlie's twin sister," Serena said. Clearly, having common sense and being chair of the Honor Board were mutually exclusive.

Lincoln sighed. "You don't trust Jackson or any of his friends, do you?"

"Of course not. Neither does Dr. Kelsey." She crossed her arms. "And neither should you."

BRADLEY MAKES AN
IMPRESSION

Mr. James pushed enough papers from his desk to clear a spot for his bowl of chicken soup. Then he leaned backward, opened his minifridge, and pulled out a jug of chocolate milk. The only good thing about the cramped security room was that he could reach his microwave, refrigerator, coffeemaker, bookshelves, file cabinets, and pegboard of keys without leaving his chair.

He hadn't always been stuck in such a small office. But when Dr. Kelsey had his newfangled security system installed, he moved Mr. James's office to a location that could accommodate all the new wires and computer equipment: the old storage closet. The room was a museum of sorts, with ancient lamps that had long since been replaced with more energy-efficient models, computer monitors that weighed more than some students, and textbooks that still referred to the USSR and a solar system with nine planets instead of eight.

Mr. James was supposed to be reviewing the footage from each camera — looking for any suspicious activity from Jackson and his friends. Without the NVR hard drive, he couldn't review all sixteen camera feeds at once, and was instead forced to pull up each camera's flash drive separately and review the video one camera at a time.

Even though Serena could be a bit pushy and melodramatic, Mr. James was glad that she had volunteered to help. They figured she could get through four of the videos a day. That still left twelve for him, and that was just during the week. Dr. Kelsey was now requiring him to come into the school over the weekend to review video then as well.

He turned off the standing lamp, allowing the large monitor to be the only light in the small room. He figured that maybe he'd take a small nap — only until his soup cooled down. He had just kicked his legs up on the desk when he heard a knock on the door.

"Mr. James, I'm so glad you're here," Megan Feldman said. Mr. James was surprised to see her. Ever since she'd quit the cheerleading squad to spend more time with the Tech Club, he hardly saw her outside the science lab.

"We need a favor," Megan continued as she motioned toward the boy behind her. Mr. James recognized him — he worked in either the guidance office or the main office, he wasn't sure. The boy's shirt and jeans were splattered with bright red paint.

"Bradley made a huge mess, but there's still a chance we can get the stains out of his clothes if we soak them now." She grabbed Bradley's arm and pulled him forward. "Can he use your office to change clothes? It'll only take a second."

Mr. James glanced down the hall, toward the boys' bathroom.

"He's a sixth grader," Megan whispered. "He's a little shy. The older boys sometimes bully him."

Mr. James took in the boy's slight frame and finally nodded. He wasn't supposed to let students into the security room, but the kid seemed harmless enough. "Just don't get any paint on my chair." *Or in my soup.* He stepped out of the room, and the boy rushed in, slamming the door behind him.

Megan adjusted her jacket and glanced at the oscillating security camera mounted on the ceiling a few feet away. It had just finished its sweep to the left. "So . . . any leads on who stole the hard drive?" she asked. "Do you think it was the same guys who flooded the school?"

Mr. James looked around the otherwise empty hallway, then stepped closer to her. He was sure that Dr. Kelsey wouldn't want him talking to anyone, and especially not one of Jackson's buddies, about the theft. But Megan had always been a trustworthy student. "To be honest, I don't know how they even broke into the security room," he said. "Not that stealing the hard drive would do them any good. It's password-protected, and no one but me and Dr. Kelsey knows the code."

"I've heard that fancy systems like that come with twenty-four-hour security monitoring." She nodded at the smartphone clipped to Mr. James's belt. "Like, you'd receive a text if someone tried to log in with a bogus password or hack into the system?"

Mr. James frowned at Megan. "You sure do know a lot about that security system —"

"I'm the president of the Tech Club," Megan said, shifting her stance. "We love everything related to computers — including security systems."

"Oh, well, yes. That makes sense." He unclipped his cell phone, then pecked in the four-digit code to unlock the screen. "Still trying to get used to this new phone. My grandkids say that it's not very advanced, but it's still better than my last one." He used a trackball and keyboard to navigate through the apps on the screen. "Anyway, it's true that there's an optional monitoring service that sends automatic updates. We had a trial version, but it ended after a month." He showed her a diagnostics screen with a bunch of numbers. "The gal from the security company tried to walk me through how to manually check if someone had hacked the system, but all that stuff went right over my head."

Megan squinted at the numbers. "Maybe I could take a look and —"

"Ah . . . I don't think that's a good idea," Mr. James said, pulling the phone away from her. "Like I told Dr. Kelsey, you can't rely on all these fancy gizmos and electric doodads. Nothing like good, old-fashioned surveillance work to get the job done."

Mr. James returned his phone to his belt, then reached into his shirt pocket and pulled out a packet of sunflower seeds. As he popped a few into his mouth, the door leading from the atrium swung open, and a couple of students slowly rolled two large recycling bins into the hallway.

Megan waved. "Hey, guys."

Mr. James frowned at the students, Wilton Jones and Carmen Cleaver. "Wilton? When did you join the Environmental Club?" Carmen wasn't a surprise, but he'd never known Wilton to be a tree hugger.

"You mean the Environmental Action Team?" Wilton positioned the bin by the wall, between the security room and the next hallway. "You know how Gaby and Carmen are," he continued. "They're good about encouraging everyone to pitch in."

"Since when do y'all put trash cans over here?" Mr. James asked.

"Recycling bins," Carmen corrected. "We received some money from an anonymous donor and were able to buy a few more bins."

Mr. James sucked on the sunflower seed in his mouth as Carmen and Wilton moved the second bin into place at the corner of the intersection of the next hallway. "Maybe they should place that one a little farther away," he said to Megan.

"Oh, I'm sure it's right where it needs to be," Megan said. "There's a science to how close together they're supposed to be placed."

"Hm, is that so?" He didn't get all the fuss about recycling. Dumping junk in the landfill had been perfectly fine for years. He didn't see any reason to stop now. "What's taking that boy so long?" Mr. James mumbled.

"I'm sure he'll be out in a second. He's got to be . . . *picture-perfect*," she said, her voice ringing through the hallway.

A second later, Hashemi Larijani popped in from around the corner. "Megan! Do you mind posing for a picture?"

Mr. James frowned. "Where's your camera, son?"

Hashemi waved the MATE. "You don't need a stand-alone camera when you have a tablet like this. The back camera has advanced zoom features and can capture up to sixty-megapixel quality in low-light settings such as —"

"Just take the picture, Hashemi," Megan said.

He held up the tablet and fiddled with the screen. After almost a minute of standing there with a fake smile plastered on his face, Mr. James asked, "Is it working? I was expecting a flash or something."

"Oh — my mistake — the app is set to video. Let me try again."

A second later, Megan and Mr. James were blinded by a barrage of flash photos.

"Got it," Hashemi said, already speeding away.

While Mr. James was still blinking, trying to readjust his eyes after the flashes, the door to the security room creaked open. "Sorry that took so long," Bradley said. "Thanks again."

As Bradley and Megan began to walk away, Mr. James glanced into his office. He noticed that the key to the security room had been placed on the wrong peg. Had he put it there by accident when he was fixing his lunch?

Then he looked down the hallway. *Maybe someone moved it.*

"Hey, son," Mr. James called. "Come on back here for a second."

Bradley hesitated, looking at Megan, then slowly returned to the security room. "Is something wrong?"

"I hate to ask this, but I'm going to need to check your clothes." He took the bag of wet clothes from Bradley. "You can't leave security to chance, you know."

The boy's face turned ashen, but he nodded. "Sure. I understand."

Mr. James quickly patted down the clothes in the bag, making sure not to get any paint on himself. "And your pockets too, if you don't mind."

Bradley emptied his pockets. "All I have is my wallet and a tin of mints." He shook the tin. "And as you can tell, it's empty."

Mr. James nodded, then handed the bag of clothes back. He must have put that key on the wrong hook when he returned to his office. Even seasoned security experts like him were prone to making a mistake every so often. "Good luck getting those stains out of your clothes. Hopefully soaking them will work."

Bradley slipped the wallet and tin back in his pockets. "Yep. Soaking. That's the key."

MAKING a LIST, CHECKING IT TWICE

Later on Thursday afternoon, after helping the basketball team to a blowout win at Wilson West, Gaby biked to Hashemi's house with Jackson. She quickly surveyed the other bikes in his backyard. She recognized all except two — though the one she was explicitly looking for wasn't there. "Where's Charlie? I thought you two talked this morning and worked everything out."

"It's complicated."

"You sound like my *tía* when she talks about her boy-friend," she said. "I just wish you and Charlie would grow up and stop fighting. As my dad likes to say, 'There's room in the coop for more than *una gallina*.'"

"Did you just call me a chicken?"

"It means that you and Charlie can coexist on the team."

"Look, I haven't kicked him off the crew. Not yet, any-way. Charlie's just . . . running through another part of the plan." He pushed up her sleeve so he could see her watch. "Come on. We're late."

"What time did the meeting start?"

"An hour ago."

Gaby slid her hat from her head. "Please don't tell me you blew off the meeting to come to my game."

"Your mom would have been lonely in the stands without me. Anyway, you were four for four from behind the arc and made eight assists. It was totally worth it." Then he winked. "As much as I would love to blame my tardiness on you, I was late on purpose. I'm trying to wait out a couple of unwanted houseguests."

"You mean Rob and Thom?" She glanced at the two bikes that she hadn't recognized earlier. "They're not going to be very happy."

"That's the point." Jackson placed his hand on the doorknob. "Thanks for looking into the deal with Eric Caan, but don't bring it up, okay? No point in getting the guys more worried than they already are."

Gaby nodded. It had taken only a few texts from a friend at Riggins to discover that Eric and his buddies had been paid to lose to Jackson and Gaby. And it hadn't been a coincidence that Eric had pushed so hard for them to meet on Saturday night. That happened to be one of the few days this month that no events were going on at Riggins — the perfect chance for Charlie and the others to scope out the school.

"I've been thinking a little more about who could be arranging all this." Gaby handed Jackson a piece of paper from her pocket. "I made a list of potential suspects."

"You're supposed to be staying out of this."

"Just think of me as a silent partner."

He opened the folded paper and looked over the names on the list. "I don't think it's Keith."

"What about Stewart Hogan or Victor Cho?"

"Stewart doesn't have the brain cells to pull this off. And Victor's not vindictive enough." Jackson smiled at the last name on the list. "And I promise it's not Lincoln Miller." He refolded the sheet and placed it in his pocket. "What, did you list everyone who we might have upset after the Election Job?"

"Seemed like a good place to start."

"I noticed you didn't mention your old flame."

"Omar was not my 'flame.' And leave him alone. He's really nice. Just not my type." Gaby took a deep breath. "You know, I've been thinking . . . Maybe you should tell Dr. Kelsey about Rob and Thom —"

"We don't have any proof," Jackson said. Any hint of a smile had disappeared. "And even if we did, we don't rat."

"Interesting how you remember that rule from the Code of Conduct, but you've forgotten the one about walking away if you're in over your head."

"I think of them more as guidelines than rules." The shed door squeaked as he pushed it open. "Ladies first."

Gaby blinked as she entered the shed. "It's like a basement in here."

"Bright lights and heat interfere with the electronics," Hashemi said as he pecked away on his laptop. Megan and Bradley sat at another table, mixing paints under a black light lamp, while Rob and Thom stood behind them, their arms crossed and faces stern.

"Finally, the Infamous Jackson Greene has graced us with his presence," Rob said once Jackson and Gaby had removed their coats. "Took you long enough."

"You're welcome to leave if you don't like waiting," Jackson said.

"Why don't you just run through your plan?" Rob said. "I don't want to be here all night."

Jackson stared at Rob for a few seconds, saying nothing, before going over to Hashemi's worktable. "Okay, Hash. Pull up the doctored video of us outside the security room and walk us through the setup. And use small words. We don't want to confuse our guests."

Hashemi punched a few keys on the laptop, bringing up the grainy, forged video of the crew breaking into the security room. "Lights. Forty percent."

The lights buzzed for a few seconds as the room darkened even more. Hashemi leaned closer to the screen. "Wow, the camera really does add ten pounds, doesn't it?"

"Just run it," Jackson said as everyone crowded around the table.

Hashemi started the video, and they watched as "Jackson" and "Hashemi" moved in and out of the security room — stealing the NVR. "From what Megan and Bradley were able to confirm, the cameras are indeed hooked up and recording. Also, according to Charlie, Serena Bianchi has volunteered to help Mr. James go through the backup video from each camera."

Rob popped his knuckles. "That brat? She'll rat us out to Dr. Kelsey the minute she figures out what we're doing."

"We'll worry about Serena later," Jackson said. "For now, we need to be able to turn off those cameras to get into Mrs. Clark's room. Any way to hack into the system remotely?"

"Sure, if I had six months and a jillion dollars' worth of equipment," Megan said. "Otherwise, the only way to turn them off is through a manual shutdown. . . . Which is almost as hard as a remote hack." She reached across Hashemi to press a few keys on the laptop. A new video screen appeared, showing the adjacent hallway. "There are two oscillating — that means rotating — cameras between the security room and the southwest storage closet, where Charlie will be hiding."

Gaby tugged her ponytail. "Wow, Kelsey really placed those cameras to get maximum coverage." She leaned closer to Bradley. "What's so important about that closet?" she whispered.

"It's our access point for sneaking into the school," Bradley said matter-of-factly. "It's the best place for Charlie to hide without getting caught."

"Charlie?" Gaby asked.

"He's our inside man," Bradley said.

Jackson pulled out his notebook and pencil. "Hash, bring in the bins."

Hashemi pressed another button, and two recycling bins popped onto the screen. "Using the video I took today, I created a simulation where we've placed the new, larger recycling bins in the strategic locations we discussed.

The bins will block enough of the hallway for Charlie to theoretically make his way to the security room undetected. Then he can unplug the cameras."

Gaby cleared her throat. "What do you mean, 'theoretically'?"

"If he's fast enough, he should be able to run to each safety point before the camera pans back to catch him. He'll have almost twenty-five seconds to get from the closet to the recycling bin at the corner of the hallway — plenty of time."

"And how much time does he have to get to the security room?" Gaby's voice was rising.

Hashemi looked at Jackson, then at Gaby. "Eight-point-two seconds. Plus or minus."

Gaby loosened her ponytail. "So you want Charlie to run through the school, dodging video cameras and hiding behind recycling bins, and break into the security room? And he only has eight-point-two seconds to run . . . what . . . seventy-five feet?"

Hashemi wiped his glasses on his shirt. "Eighty-four feet."

"We thought about trying to hide Charlie in one of the bins tomorrow afternoon, but it's too risky — there's a chance someone could open it and blow his cover," Jackson said.

Gaby stared at the screen again. Jackson had promised that he'd look after Charlie. That he'd keep him out of trouble. "Do you have to go in at night?"

"We checked the school schedule," Jackson said.

"There's too much going on during the day. Nighttime gives us the most flexibility." He put his hand on her shoulder and gave it a small squeeze. "Don't worry. Charlie can do it. He's a pro."

Rob pushed his way past Bradley so that he was standing beside Jackson. "What about the *test*?"

Jackson glared at Rob. "Once Charlie disables the cameras, the rest of us will enter the school through Mrs. Cooper's room — she always leaves her window unlocked. We'll install a device that'll allow us to power on and off the cameras remotely and gather the rest of the information we need. We'll sneak back in next week, once Mrs. Clark has developed the exam, and get the answers."

"I don't like your plan," Rob said. "But we'll go along with it for now." He walked to the door, with Thom trailing closely behind. "And Jackson, don't try anything funny. We still have that video."

After Rob and Thom left, Megan slapped the table. A few loose wires bounced in the air. "I really can't stand those guys."

"Don't worry, they'll get what's coming to them — Rob, Thom, *and* their mastermind," Jackson said. "You sure you guys will be able to download the video from the cameras tomorrow? That footage is our best chance at figuring out who's behind this."

Megan nodded. "Once we're physically plugged into the cameras, it shouldn't be a problem."

"Good." Jackson looked at the table with the paints. "And how's the ink coming along?"

"We were able to successfully mix the fluorescent ink and the invisible ink," Bradley said. "But we're still working on the timing."

"And the watches?" Jackson asked Hashemi.

"They're in beta —"

Everyone groaned.

"— but I should have all three ready by next week."

Jackson cocked his head. "Three?"

Hashemi nodded. "Rob and Thom asked for an extra."

Jackson made a note. "Sounds like the mastermind needs one as well. That narrows things down."

"What about transportation?" Gaby asked. "You can't just bike up there on Friday night."

"Already got it covered," Jackson said. "Samuel's getting Ray Basilone to shuttle us around in his van. Should be enough room for all of us and whatever equipment we need."

Megan leaned against the table. "Just as a reminder, even if your ultimate plan works and we're able to get Rob and Thom and whoever to hand over the forged video, there's nothing stopping them from turning us in anyway. They could buy another hard drive, have Kayla the Cheat load up another copy of the video, and drop it off at school."

"They don't even have to buy a new one," Hashemi said. "They can use the hard drive from Kayla's machine."

"Kayla the Cheat's machine," Megan corrected. "Might as well be her middle name." She cleared her throat. "But you know, I've been tinkering with a password-decoding program. We could sneak into Kayla the Cheat's house and —"

"Megan . . ." Jackson began.

"It's just an option," she said. "I wanted to toss it out there in case this plan doesn't work."

"That's our problem," Jackson said. "All of our options are bad options. Just too many variables. . . ." He tried to stick his pencil behind his ear, but it kept falling out of place. Finally, he tossed it on the table. "Okay, let's pack it up for tonight. Tomorrow's a big day."

Gaby swept her hair back from her face and watched as Jackson pulled her list of potential masterminds from his jacket. He walked off, still muttering to himself, while the others remained at the table.

"What's with Jackson?" Megan asked Gaby. "I've never seen him so nervous before."

Gaby shrugged, then walked away too. She knew she should have responded, but she didn't want to tell Megan the truth.

Jackson wasn't nervous. He was scared.

EXECUTIVE ORDERS

Gaby entered her house, dropped her book bag off on the kitchen table, and walked down the hallway. She knocked on her brother's bedroom door, but after no one answered, she continued on to her parents' room. Her father was lying on the bed, an empty plate beside him.

"*¡Mija!*" he yelled before blowing her a kiss. "I can't believe I missed your game. I heard you were amazing! Twelve points — all threes!"

"I was just open," Gaby said.

"And what about all those assists? I can't wait to tell the guys at the station —"

"Lynne and LaKisha happened to be in the right place at the right time every time I passed them the ball," Gaby said, loosening her ponytail. "And please don't brag. Knowing me, I'll have a horrible game next week."

He snorted. "Nonsense. And I'm your *papi*. It's my job to brag." He took a sip from a bottle of water. "According to your mother, I haven't been the only one bragging."

Gaby felt her face warm. "Yes, Jackson was cheering. Like everyone else."

"You know, you can invite him over. I don't bite."

"Daddy, the last time he was here, you started cleaning your hunting knife."

"It was a joke," he said. "Jackson was supposed to laugh, not run for the door."

"He's nervous. He wants you to like him."

"*Mija*," he said. "I wouldn't let you date him if I didn't like him."

Gaby's face went from warm to blazing. "So . . . Where's Mom and Charlie?"

"Your mother had to run to the grocery store but should be home soon. Carlito is outside, running around like a chicken with its head cut off." He glanced at his alarm clock. "Go tell him it's time to come in. It's getting late, and he's probably freezing."

She nodded, closed his door, and went out to the back-yard. Even though most of the snow had melted, Charlie was able to pile enough of it together to form what looked like a ragged, uneven maze.

"Watch your step," he said as she walked toward him. "You're about to plow through the boys' bathroom."

Gaby sat down at the picnic table. "How long have you been out here?"

He sat down next to her. "Long enough to lose the feeling in my fingers."

"Charlie . . ."

"I'm kidding. Mostly." He glanced at his watch — *Jackson's* watch, she noticed — then tapped the notepad on top of the table. "I'm close. I can almost make that eighty-foot dash. Just need to shave off one more second."

"Eighty-four feet," Gaby corrected.

Charlie rolled his eyes. "So you know the plan too?"

"Jackson told me this afternoon." She glanced at all the times scribbled on the notebook page. "Maybe you've practiced enough. You're going to be sore."

"One. More. Second." He licked his dry, ragged lips. "My mouth's going to look like sandpaper tomorrow." He winked. "At least I'm not kissing anyone."

"Not funny." The last person she wanted to discuss kissing with was her brother. "I didn't come out here to talk about me and Jackson. I came to talk about *you* and Jackson."

"Not interested in a lecture."

"Too bad," Gaby said. "I know you and Jackson aren't talking. Not really."

"He knows where to find me."

"It's not like you're making it easy for him to trust you." She yanked the notebook from him so he'd have to look at her. "I mean, really — switching the meeting location was childish."

"How many times do I have to apologize for that?"

Gaby took a deep breath. "I'm sorry. I didn't come out here to argue either. I just want you two to talk. I've never seen him this stumped before." She placed her hand on Charlie's arm. "Maybe you guys should walk away. It's too risky."

"That's not going to happen."

"Then talk to him. Help him improve the plan. He'll listen to you."

"I tried."

"Try again." She reached up and tugged on a piece of hair poking out from underneath his hat. "And if it helps, you've always been better at video games than Jackson."

"Not that I've played a whole bunch lately. You and Jackson hogged the best game."

"That's just because we were practicing for our show-down with Eric Caan."

"Convenient," Charlie mumbled. "So what was the excuse before that? Y'all were studying for the American history exam? Playing basketball at the Fitz?"

Gaby crossed her arms. "Are you jealous?"

"No way. Of course not." He glanced at the snow maze. "But it's hard to play a two-person video game when neither your best friend nor your twin sister is ever around."

Gaby looked at Charlie, but he wouldn't meet her gaze. She and Jackson *had* been spending a lot of time together. Maybe too much. . . .

"Charlie. I'm —"

"Forget it," he said. "So are you just here to give me advice, or has Jackson recruited you as well?"

"I can't get involved. I'll help as much as I can, but —"

"No, that's good. No point in getting pulled into this mess."

She read the times listed on the notepad, then pushed it toward him. "You really want to do this run tomorrow?"

"I have to. And not just because I want to prove some-thing to Jackson."

"Okay." She touched her dry lips. She'd left her lip balm in her book bag on the table. "We've got about thirty minutes before the sun goes down completely. Let's get to it."

"What?"

"You're fast, but only because of your genes," she said. "If you had ever bothered to learn how to run the right way, you'd be even faster. So I'm going to teach you." She pointed to the watch on his arm. "Hand it over."

"Gaby —"

"Stop talking and save your breath," she said. "You're going to need it."

GABY AND THE BRICK WALL

As soon as Gaby arrived at school on Friday morning, she made a beeline for the main office. She had been up most of the night before, thinking through Jackson's plan. Jackson believed the camera footage gave them the best chance at determining the identity of the mastermind. But Gaby figured it was worth talking to one more source.

She caught Dr. Kelsey just as he was about to start his rounds. "Hello, Ms. de la Cruz," he said as he closed his office door behind him. "My, you look fancy this morning."

Gaby knew he was talking about the red lipstick she was wearing. She didn't like it, but it was the only color that adequately hid her horribly raw lips. "I just wanted to check on the status of the carpeting," she said. She had practiced what she was going to say, but now that she was here, nerves were beginning to take over.

"They should be able to replace it in a couple of weeks," he said.

"That fast?"

He nodded. "It's not quite what I wanted, but it'll have to do," he said. "Although our insurance will cover most of the repair costs, I'd hoped that some of our more affluent donors would have contributed to a few upgrades I wanted to make. Unfortunately, that didn't happen."

He had to be talking about Keith's father. Keith had let everyone know that his dad refused to donate any more money to the school — not until there were some "changes in management."

"Well, I'm glad it'll be fixed soon." Then she took a breath. No point in beating around the bush. "Just being curious, have you learned anything else about who's behind the pranks?"

His eyes sparkled. "Why? Are you here to tell me something about your brother's involvement?"

Gaby crossed her arms. "Charlie didn't have anything to do with it. You practically said so yourself when you decided not to take him before the Honor Board."

"No, I said I couldn't *prove* that he was involved. Big difference." He tugged on his coat. "Charlie by himself isn't smart enough to pull off something like that — no offense. But I wouldn't put *anything* past him and Jackson Greene working together." He turned and looked at the door to the copy room. "I'm still trying to figure out how they pulled off that stunt during the Fall Formal."

"Alleged stunt," she whispered.

"What was that?" he asked, stepping toward her.

"Nothing — just that I'm positive that neither Jackson nor Charlie had anything to do with the flooding prank."

"How can you be so sure?"

You mean, other than being with Jackson while the school was being flooded? Other than knowing that they've been framed?

But instead of saying that, she replied, "Don't you think it could be someone else?"

"Nonsense. The only other student cavalier enough to pull something like that was Keith. And according to his father, Keith was home the entire night."

"There are plenty of other sneaky, slimy students at Maplewood," Gaby said. She almost wished she had a copy of her list to show to him.

"You mean like members of the Tech Club? The Art Geeks? The school newspaper?" Dr. Kelsey glanced at his watch. "Let me give you some free advice — you can't choose who your family is, but you can always pick your friends. And Jackson Greene is not the type of boy you should be spending your time with."

"Why? He didn't do anything wrong!"

"Or maybe he just didn't get caught," he said. "He's a criminal. It's in his blood." He walked toward the door. "No one is above the rules of this school, Ms. de la Cruz, no matter how popular he or she may be. As Student Council president, I expect you to alert me if you know of *anyone's* involvement. Even your friends or family."

No, Gaby thought. *My job is to stand up for all students. Especially my friends and family.*

She exited the office and headed toward Jackson's locker. He looked up as she approached. "You look really nice this morning," he said. Then he frowned. "And really angry."

"I confirmed with Dr. Kelsey — the new carpeting won't be installed for a few more weeks, so you don't have to worry about crews in the hallways this week or next."

"Yeah, Bradley told me that yesterday, but thanks for double-checking." He closed his locker and started to walk off, but paused when he realized Gaby wasn't following. "What? Is something else wrong?"

"You sure Ray's driving his van tonight?" After Jackson nodded, she said, "Good. You just got an extra passenger."

THE RUNNING MAN

Three hours after the last bell of the school week had rung, Charlie de la Cruz sat in the corner of the storage closet, pressed between stacks of long fluorescent lights and old dusty mops. The clipboard holding all of Mr. Hutton's maintenance requests jutted into the top of his head, and he was sure that the bucket sitting a few feet away from him hadn't been cleaned in months.

Charlie applied another coat of lip balm. Gaby had worked him hard last night, helping him shave off that one last second, but it came at the cost of his nose and lips.

Jackson's shiny silver watch beeped on his arm. Six o'clock. A few moments later, his earpiece crackled to life. "The school's been empty for almost an hour," Jackson said. "You ready?"

Charlie spoke into the microphone clipped to his shirt, wondering if the rest of the team was listening in. "I've been thinking — the cameras' flash drives record over themselves after twenty-four hours, right? So even if I get caught on video, it'll record over itself by Monday morning. So maybe I don't have to worry so much about the cameras."

"Technically, you're correct," Jackson said. "That's why we're going in today. But I'd bet all the money in Hash's piggy bank that Dr. Kelsey or Mr. James will be in this weekend to check the video — it's what I would do. So stop thinking and get ready to run."

Charlie sighed. *Good thing I ate my Wheaties this morning.*

"Even though we can't see what you're doing, we'll be keeping time here as well, and I'll let you know when to run and when to stop." Jackson mumbled a few words at someone else in the van, then said, "Forty-five seconds, Charlie."

Charlie stood up and rattled the door handle. It seemed colder and smoother than usual. Had it always been this way, or had he never noticed? He braced his other hand against the doorframe. He and Gaby had decided that the best strategy was to catapult himself out of the door. Not that the first leg of the run was all that difficult — he wouldn't have any problem making it to the first recycling bin in time. Reaching the security room would be another matter. He'd practiced the run almost fifty times and had made it under eight seconds only twice.

"Get ready. . . ." Jackson said into his ear. "And . . . Go!"

Charlie launched himself into the hallway, jumping so far that he almost crashed into the wall ahead of him. He spun to his right and sped to the large green recycling bin in the corner. As soon as he reached it, he dropped to his knees, tucked himself behind it, and checked his watch. Fourteen seconds.

"Charlie . . . ?"

"I'm here," he replied. He hoped Jackson couldn't tell how shaky his voice sounded. "No sweat."

"Okay, sit tight. You've got about a minute and a half until your next window."

The hardest part about the second leg of the run was that he had to be out of view of *both* cameras before he could move — limiting him to that window of 8.2 seconds. Give or take.

The watch beeped again. Charlie moved into position. "How much time till I go?" he asked.

"Fifteen seconds," Jackson said. Then, an eternity later: "Five . . . four . . . three . . . two . . . one . . . Go!"

Charlie exploded from his crouch and flew toward the security door, counting the time through clenched teeth. The second recycling bin grew larger in his view, bouncing from left to right with each frantic step.

He dropped behind it but didn't dare look at his watch. "Jackson . . . ?" he muttered, trying to control his breathing. "Did I . . . make it?"

"Nine-point-eight seconds," Jackson said.

Charlie's heart sank.

"So I guess it's a good thing we built in a few extra seconds," Jackson continued.

"Wait. What?" Charlie took in a few deeps breaths before starting again. "You mean . . . I made it?"

"You actually had a window of fourteen seconds, but we didn't tell you that. We thought a smaller window might motivate you a bit more."

Megan's voice came into his ear. "And we had to punish you at least a little for lying to us about the Trophy Heist."

Charlie could hear everyone else in the background, laughing and cheering. He wanted to be mad, but he also knew he probably deserved it. "You guys . . ."

"You're not out of the woods yet," Jackson said. "Your window to unlock the security room just started. You've got twenty-five seconds."

Charlie stood, shook out his cramping legs, and unlocked the door. It was only after he turned on the lights that he allowed himself to smile. "Unplugging the cameras now."

"Okay, we'll move into position."

Gaby had barely closed the van door before Samuel and his friend Ray Basilone sped off down the road, a puff of exhaust smoke trailing behind them. They had promised to return in an hour. She readjusted her black backpack and joined the rest of the crew. Everyone seemed happy — thrilled, even — that Charlie had made it to the room, but the way she saw it, they had all dodged a huge bullet. It should have been her inside the building, not Charlie. There was no question that she was the best sprinter in the group, and she was in the best shape. But the only way

Jackson and Charlie had agreed to let her join the crew was if she dropped her request to take Charlie's place.

That seemed to be the only thing they agreed on.

They walked along the edge of the campus toward the back of the school, with tall, snow-capped cedars on one side and a bare parking lot on the other. They stopped at a row of picnic tables just outside the camera's perimeter. "Bradley, reach into my bag and hand me those binoculars," Jackson said.

"What do you need those for?" Gaby asked.

"The cameras aren't supposed to have internal batteries, but given how much Kelsey paid for the system, you can never be too sure." He brought the binoculars to his face. "If they're really off, then the rotating camera outside of the gym will be stationary." After a second, he passed the binoculars back to Bradley, then spoke into his microphone. "Good job, Charlie. We're heading to the rendezvous point now."

Jackson started toward the building, his feet following an already worn path through the slushy parking lot. Gaby sped up to catch him, leaving the others behind.

"Tell me the truth," she said. "Did you really think Charlie was going to make it to the security room in time?"

A small smile spread on Jackson's face. "Honestly, I had no idea."

"And you let him do it anyway?"

Jackson stopped walking. "He knew the risks."

"He only did it because he's trying to compete with you," she said. "I don't know what's going on between you two, but stroking your ego isn't worth putting him in danger."

"Gaby . . ." Jackson's voice trailed off as the others approached.

Bradley pulled his scarf down from his mouth. "Something wrong?"

"We're fine," Jackson mumbled, looking at the ground. "Go on ahead. We'll be there in a second."

Even though it was windy, Gaby swore someone — probably Megan — said, "Sounds like trouble in paradise."

"Be honest," she said. "Why did you make him do the run?"

"I didn't *make* him do anything," Jackson said, shaking his head. "Why are we talking about this? I don't see what the problem —"

"You should have let me do it!" she said. "You know I could have made it in fourteen seconds without a problem. I could have made it in eight seconds." She crossed her arms. "I'm not some helpless, defenseless girl, just tagging along to be with her boyfriend."

Jackson's mouth dropped open, and Gaby realized what she'd said. What she'd called him.

He tilted his head a little to the left. "I'm . . . your boyfriend?"

"No. I mean, yeah. I mean . . ." She tugged her hat lower over her ears. "Don't you want to be?"

Jackson quickly nodded. "Yes. Of course. I just thought . . . You never called me that —"

"You could have called me that too —"

"And then you never gave me a chance to kiss you."

"What?" She rolled her eyes. "What are you even talking about?"

"You've never given me an opening — an opportunity — to kiss you. I wasn't sure if you wanted me to or not."

Gaby took a deep breath. She was glad it was dark outside. It made it easier to talk. "Jackson Greene, we see each other every day. We email every night. Of course I want to kiss you."

"Well, the rules say that the girl is supposed to give the guy the signal —"

"Rules?"

"Yeah." Jackson's face looked red, and she wasn't sure if it was from the cold or from embarrassment. "Samuel's Rules of Romance."

"Jackson! The last time you took your brother's advice about girls, we didn't speak for four months!"

"But the rules say —"

"Jackson, trust me." She took a step forward. "Forget the rules."

Then Gaby closed her eyes and waited.

And waited. And waited.

Finally, she opened her eyes again. "Jackson. Seriously?"

Jackson wasn't looking at her. Instead, he was focused on the school. "I think we're being watched."

Gaby turned around. While Charlie helped Megan climb into Mrs. Cooper's room, Hashemi and Bradley stood against the wall, staring at her and Jackson. Hashemi might even have been recording them with the MATE. "Your crew . . ."

"Hey, they're your crew now too," Jackson said. He tugged on her ponytail, and she turned back around. "See, this is why you should always plan things out."

She laughed, because that was about all she could do. "To be honest, my lips are really chapped. They hurt a lot. And they're kind of gross." She sighed. "But still consider me open for a kiss. Anytime. Just not when we have an audience. . . ."

"Or when it's freezing outside. . . ."

"Or when we're trying to disable the security system and sneak into the school," she said. "Even though I still think I should have been the one inside."

Before Gaby realized it, Jackson had taken her hand. Even through the gloves, she swore she could feel his pulse. "Come on," he said. "Let me show you something."

The rest of the crew had already made it into Mrs. Cooper's room by the time Jackson and Gaby reached the open window. Everyone inside was smiling and laughing. Even Megan grinned as she punched Charlie's shoulder, then patted him on the back.

"Allowing Charlie to make the run didn't have anything to do with protecting you," Jackson said. "It was his way of saying he was sorry."

Once inside, the crew returned to the security room. Hashemi pointed to a mass of unplugged Ethernet cables, then followed them with his finger as they disappeared behind a bookshelf. He nudged the bookshelf out of the way, exposing a large white plastic cover at the base of the wall. The sixteen Ethernet cables, each affixed with a small tag, snaked through a large hole molded into the plastic.

Hashemi knelt in front of the wall and began unfastening the first of eight screws. "They labeled each cable," he said. "That should speed things up."

"Are you sure your circuit breaker is going to work?" Charlie asked.

"Please call it the Pikachu," Hashemi said. "It deserves to be respected."

"Did you actually say that with a straight face?" Charlie asked.

"What?" Megan nudged him. "Not as catchy as 'The Great Greene Heist'?"

Bradley raised his hand. "I thought we were calling it the Election Job again."

Charlie pulled Bradley's hand back down, then looked at Hashemi. "All I'm saying is, that's a pretty fancy name for a device held together by duct tape."

"Gorilla Tape," Hashemi replied. "And that's only because I didn't have time to solder the unit closed."

"I just hope it's small enough to fit back there, and that the wireless radio will transmit through the wall." Megan pulled the small, piecemeal device from her bag. She and Hashemi had had to abandon work on the RhinoBot for a few days, but with specs they found online and a bit of creative engineering, they had been able to quickly construct the Pikachu, a crude circuit breaker. If it worked, they'd be able to power the cameras on and off remotely.

Hashemi loosened the last screw, then removed the wall plate, exposing a large, ragged square hole. He pressed a few buttons on his watch, turning on a wide neon-blue beam of light on the side of the case. He pointed the light toward the hole. "We should have plenty of room."

"Isn't that light a little too strong?" Gaby asked. "I thought the plan was to get Rob and Thom to use those watches during the test, so we could trick them into using Bradley's disappearing ink."

"That *is* the plan." Jackson sighed. "Hash, try to cut back on the wattage, okay? It's not a Bat-Signal. It needs to *leak* light." Jackson glanced at his watch, recently retrieved from Charlie's sweaty arm. "Are you guys sure we'll be able to monitor whether the cameras are drawing power?"

Megan opened her laptop. "We'll do a run-through after we get it installed."

"Good." Jackson picked two rings of keys from the pegboard on the wall. "These should be the master keys," he said. "Bradley and I will check out Mrs. Clark's file cabinet while Charlie and Gaby take the measurements for the two cameras in the social studies wing."

"We don't need the measurements anymore," Hashemi said. "We have the Pikachu."

Jackson picked up the device and smoothed a piece of tape back into place. "Um . . . Let's go ahead and map out the locations and viewing angles of the cameras anyway. Just to be on the safe side."

"I don't understand what you guys are talking about," Charlie said. "Why do you need to map the cameras?"

"Can you fill Charlie in?" Jackson asked Gaby. "I need to get started. There's no telling how long it'll take to find the right keys to Mrs. Clark's door and file cabinet."

Gaby nodded, then Jackson and Bradley exited the room. "Maybe I should go with Gaby," Bradley said as they walked toward the atrium. "It might take a while for her to explain the plan to Charlie."

Jackson shook his head. "I need you with me. I've got a special assignment just for you."

"Sure. No problem." They continued in silence, though Jackson could tell that Bradley wanted to say something. Finally, the younger boy blurted out, "I have to ask — what happened out there? Why didn't you kiss her?"

"Um, maybe because I didn't want an audience?"

"I *knew* you could see me and Hashemi," he said. "Now I owe Charlie ten bucks."

"You guys were betting on me? And Charlie bet *against* me?"

"He says that you're too much of a perfectionist to just kiss her. You have to plan it out. Make it perfect. But I was sure it was going to happen, especially when I saw her with all that lipstick today. . . ."

"Apparently, she has chapped lips. She says they hurt."

"That makes sense," Bradley said. "I've kissed a girl when my lips were really chapped. It does kind of hurt. And no one wants their first kiss to be in front of a bunch of people."

Jackson stopped walking. "You've kissed a girl before?"

"Girls," Bradley said, stressing the s. "First time was at my cousin's Bat Mitzvah last year. She was older too. Fourteen. Practically a woman."

"But . . . How did you know she wanted you to kiss her? Did she give you a sign or something?"

"She said, 'Bradley, kiss me.' Does that count?"

"I should know better than to talk to a sixth grader about romance." Jackson walked a few more steps, then asked, "So which way do you turn your head when you do it?"

Once at Mrs. Clark's classroom, Jackson quickly found the master key that opened the door. "You're lucky," he said as they slipped inside. "The rumor is that she's retiring next year. You'll get to escape the wrath of Clark." He pulled the second set of keys from his bag. "Hopefully one of these will work on the file cabinet."

The lock popped open on the tenth key.

"Here's where you come in," Jackson said, walking away from the file cabinet. "I need you to look through each drawer and see where she keeps her tests."

"Why me?"

He sighed. "Sixth graders. So many questions."

"At least I've kissed a girl."

Jackson grinned. "Score one for Bradley. Now go ahead. I'll make molds of the keys while you're looking."

Bradley began flipping through the files, but it wasn't long before he found what he was looking for. "Jackson . . ." He pulled out a green folder. "I think this is the test."

Jackson placed the key mold on a desk as Bradley crossed the room. Bradley started to open the folder, but Jackson turned away and snapped his eyes shut. "Don't open it. At least, not where I can see inside." He took a step away. "Does the test have next Friday's date on it?"

"Yeah."

"Fifty questions? And it's multiple choice?" Jackson continued.

"Yes and yes," Bradley said. "Did you know she'd already have the final exam done?"

"I suspected it. That's one of the reasons I was glad Rob and Thom decided not to come with us."

"Are we going to make copies for them?"

Jackson shook his head. "First, it wouldn't do any good. They wouldn't trust anything we gave them — they'll want to see the exam in the file cabinet with their own eyes. And second, even if they somehow believed us, I don't want to give them the answers this early. Rob and Thom may be idiots, but even they can memorize fifty answers by next week." He picked up the key mold and pressed the room key into the clay. "But if we give them the answers the night before the exam . . ."

"They won't have time to memorize it. They'll be forced to use the disappearing ink."

"Hopefully," Jackson said. "There are still a lot of unknown variables."

Bradley returned the folder to the file cabinet. "That's why you wanted me to come with you. So you wouldn't accidentally see the test."

"Other than Megan, you're the only one of us not taking Mrs. Clark's class." Jackson removed the key from the clay and then inspected the imprint. "We may be thieves, but we're not cheats."

HIDE aND SEEK

Back in the security room, Megan had almost finished updating the monitoring software on her laptop when it started beeping. She brought up the diagnostics tab. The sixteen icons representing the cameras were slowly fading from gray to red. "Hashemi! Unplug the Pikachu! The cameras are powering up."

"But it's not plugged in," he said. He put down his screwdriver and held up the plug. "See?"

"Then we've got a problem," she mumbled as she wiggled the long black USB cord connecting her laptop to the Pikachu.

"Maybe your program has a glitch."

She snorted. "Next option." She glanced at the device. All sixteen cameras were attached. "Are you sure that thing has to be plugged into an electrical socket to work? You didn't try to stick the RhinoBot battery in there, did you?"

"Of course I didn't — though I considered it briefly. But anyway, no, there's no way those cameras should be drawing power from the Pikachu. . . ." Hashemi's voice trailed off as he and Megan looked at each other. "But that doesn't mean the power isn't coming from somewhere else."

She turned on her microphone. "Jackson and Charlie — where are you?"

"Bradley and I are still in Mrs. Clark's room," Jackson replied.

"And Gaby and I are still taking measurements," Charlie said. "Why?"

"You need to get out of the hallway." She gulped in a breath of air. "The cameras are powering on."

"Wait — you mean they're recording?" Jackson yelped. "Can you turn them back off?"

"I don't know," Megan said. "They aren't supposed to be on in the first place."

She glanced at her laptop screen. One of the cameras — the one outside of the football field — had just turned green. It was recording.

"Charlie! Get inside Mrs. Clark's room!" she yelled. "Now."

She immediately heard loud, hurried steps through her earpiece. A few seconds later, a door slammed shut. "Charlie and Gaby just got here," Jackson said. "Did they get caught on camera?"

Megan stared at the screen as the first interior camera powered on. "I think they made it."

On the other side of the school, Jackson stood in front of Mrs. Clark's smudged chalkboard, his hand pressed against the earpiece shoved into his ear. Bradley stood beside him, furiously waving both sets of key molds to speed up their drying. Gaby and Charlie leaned against the wall and tried to catch their breaths.

"Any idea what's going on?" Jackson asked. "Are you sure the Pikachu didn't trigger the cameras?"

"Positive," Hashemi said. "We think there's another device that can turn on the cameras. Maybe it's a backup system of some kind."

"I just ran an advanced network scan," Megan said. "There's definitely another switch physically attached to the cameras. The connection is too strong and stable."

Jackson rapped the top of Mrs. Clark's desk. "A backup system? Are you sure? None of our intelligence even remotely pointed to something like this existing, let alone being installed here." He turned to Gaby. "Kelsey hasn't had any work done on the security system this week, has he?"

"Not that I'm aware of," she said. "The way I understand it, the superintendent didn't want the KRX Supreme system installed in the first place, and isn't about to pay for any additional upgrades or service."

Jackson checked his watch. "Okay, forget the other system for a second. Is there any way to wipe the camera video remotely using the Pikachu?"

"Negative," Hashemi said. "It's only made to monitor power levels and to turn on and off any devices attached to it."

"Does the Pikachu even still work with that other mystery device attached to the cameras?" Gaby asked. "And will the backup system — if that's what it really

123

is — power the cameras on as soon as you try to turn them off?"

Jackson repeated the questions to Megan. After a few seconds, she said, "The cameras were off for twenty-three minutes before they switched back on. My gut feeling is that, if it's an automated backup system, it's got some built-in lapse time. If not, it would have turned on immediately when Charlie unplugged the cameras." She sighed. "But that's a guess. There's only one real way to find out."

"Maybe we should get out of here before something else goes wrong." Gaby placed her hand on Jackson's arm. "It's not like we have another choice."

Instead of replying, Jackson stared at the smudged chalkboard. "Where did you guys find those plans for the Pikachu again?"

"On an online forum we belong to," Hashemi said.

"And you didn't have to modify it?" Jackson asked.

"Just minor tweaks," Megan said. "We already had most of the parts."

Jackson rubbed his face. "This is too much of a coincidence."

"Maybe Gaby's right," Bradley said, the key molds still in his hand. "Maybe we should sort all this out once we're outside."

"We're almost finished on our end," Megan said. "We can switch off the cameras whenever you're ready."

Jackson continued to stare at the board. *Too many coincidences. . . .*

"Jackson?" Megan's voice was loud and sharp in his earpiece. "Did you copy that?"

"Hold up on turning off those cameras," he said.

"Why?"

"What if it's not some automated system?" Jackson began pacing the room. "What if it's someone sitting at a computer — with a monitoring system just like yours — who's waiting to turn those cameras back on as soon as you turn them off?"

"But if that was the case, they should have powered them back on as soon as we turned them off the first time," Megan said.

"Perhaps," Jackson said. "Another question: What's the lag time from the cameras powering on to being fully functional?"

"Pulling up the diagnostics. . . . It took about thirty to forty-five seconds last time. Sooner for the ones outside — they're more powerful because of the need for night vision. The ones inside have older processors and take longer to boot up."

Jackson looked at Charlie, who was still slumped against the wall. He had avoided asking for Charlie's opinion since the operation began, mostly so he wouldn't have to deal with any possible attitude. But that suddenly seemed silly. "What do you think?" he asked.

Charlie twisted a short tuft of his hair. Jackson wasn't sure if he was thinking or hesitating. Finally, he said, "We're close to Mrs. Cooper's room, so we'd have a shot at making it back before the cameras start recording. But there's no way Hashemi and Megan would reach us. Not in forty-five seconds." He stepped toward Jackson. "But you don't think it's a security system backup, do you?"

Jackson shook his head. "We're being played. There are just too many coincidences." He picked up his microphone. "Megan, do you think Kayla could be behind this?"

After another few seconds of silence, Megan said, "I suppose she could figure out a way to set up a system like the Pikachu. And then Rob and Thom could have installed it when they broke into the school and stole the NVR's hard drive."

"If it really is Kayla, maybe we can wait her out," Bradley said, still waving the molds. "She has to go to bed eventually. She can't turn the cameras off if she's asleep."

"Kayla could have set up the cameras to automatically power on in her absence," Megan said. "It's what I would have done."

"Well, I don't want to hang around until midnight, hoping she falls asleep," Jackson said. "I'm guessing that wouldn't go over so well with our parents." He smiled at Gaby, but she wasn't smiling back. "What's wrong?"

"We've got another problem." Gaby pointed to the rings of keys on one of the desks. "We have to return the masters to the security room."

"It's bad enough if we get caught on video sneaking out of the school," Charlie said. "But if Kelsey knows we have the master keys . . ."

"So now what?" Megan asked. "We sit here and wait to be caught?"

"The good thing is, we're not in any immediate danger," Jackson said. "Hash, make sure you finish the setup on the Pikachu. If we ever get out of here, I want to be able to monitor those cameras. And Megan, I still want you to download the video from all the cameras to a flash drive. Then see if you can figure out a way to shut down those cameras for a little longer. But I need minutes, not seconds."

"I've got an idea," Megan said, "but Hashemi's not going to like it."

"Acknowledged. Will call back in a bit." Jackson turned off his microphone, then motioned for Charlie to do the same. "Whoever is behind this is smart."

"Too smart," Charlie added. "This isn't something he or she just thought about tonight."

Jackson led him to the farthest window, away from the others. "I think Kayla planted the schematics for the Pikachu. I think she wanted us to find them and use them to sneak in."

"That's crazy," Charlie said.

"Okay, let's start at the beginning and talk this through," Jackson said. "I didn't tell the others about this, but I'm pretty sure I was set up so I wouldn't have an alibi on Saturday night. The same night you and the crew snuck into Riggins."

"But even if you were set up, how would they know I was going to case Riggins the same day? I only told the crew, and I know they didn't tell anyone."

"Did you write it down? In the red notebook they stole from your locker?"

Charlie nodded. "Okay, fair enough. So it wasn't a coincidence that we didn't have alibis. But what does that have to do with us being stuck here tonight?"

Jackson pulled his pencil from behind his ear and tapped it against his palm. "Back to your locker. . . . They broke into it and swiped your messenger bag and the notebook. But how did they get the combination to the padlock? More importantly, how did they know the bag and the notebook were there in the first place?"

Charlie leaned against the window. He had always been wary of the camera positioned outside of his locker — at times it seemed like it was focused directly on him. But he had told himself not to worry about it, because Dr. Kelsey already knew the combination to his padlock. He didn't need to review a video to get it.

"The cameras," Charlie said. "You think the mastermind found a way to monitor and control them."

"It's the only explanation that makes sense. If they had access to the cameras, they could easily track what you were putting in your locker. They could get your combination by zooming in as you opened the padlock."

Charlie ran his fingers through his hair. "I bet that's how they knew about the meeting in the newsroom."

"And the text message they delivered to Gaby on Monday — how else would they know I was standing next to her?" Jackson shook his head. "I was so happy when Rob and Thom said they weren't coming with us today. That way, we could set everything up without them knowing." He looked down at the notebook in his jacket pocket. "I thought they were scared of getting caught. . . . But maybe they were never supposed to come in the first place. Maybe —"

"What are you two talking about?" Gaby asked as she

and Bradley joined them. "Are you figuring out a way to get us out of this mess?"

Charlie glanced out the window. "More like, figuring out how bad of a mess we're in."

"I've been all wrong about this," Jackson mumbled to himself. "How could I be so stupid? This isn't about the exam. It's never been about the exam."

"Without the answers, Rob and Thom fail," Bradley said.

"But they aren't the ones calling the shots," Jackson said. "Think about it — what's better than a fake video of a break-in?"

Charlie sighed. "A real one."

"Exactly. Our mastermind doesn't *only* want the answers to the exam. He wants revenge. He wants to see us humiliated. He wants to catch us in the act. On video. And we just played right into his hands."

They all remained silent for a few seconds, letting this new revelation sink in.

As Charlie stared at his shoes, he wondered if they would have figured this out sooner if he'd been more honest with Jackson.

A few feet away, Jackson wondered if they could have avoided this mess if he had talked to Charlie like Gaby had asked him to.

"Dude," Charlie said.

"I know," Jackson replied. "I should have —"

"Me too."

They both took a deep breath, then smiled. "So we're good?" Jackson asked.

Charlie nodded. "We're good."

Gaby stepped between the two boys. "Hold on. Did you two make up? Just like that?"

"Yeah," Charlie said. "Isn't that what you wanted?"

She crossed her arms. "I had this big speech planned out. . . ."

"Don't worry — I'm sure Charlie and I will fight again. Save it for then. First things first." Jackson turned his microphone back on. "Megan, you still there?"

"Duh."

"Have you figured out how to buy us some more time?"

"I have an idea. But it's a stretch." There was a pause as she rustled through some papers. "We could infect the Pikachu with malware."

"Because both the NVR and the cameras have their own storage systems, CPU, et cetera," Hashemi said, "the KRX Supreme's operating system has security measures in place to limit and compartmentalize damage. If there's some type of threat, the entire system shuts down, which protects any unaffected pieces until a fix is installed."

"How long would that buy us?" Jackson asked.

"If Kayla's monitoring us, she should be able to upload a patch pretty quickly," Megan said. "It'll take about three to four minutes for the fix to start working."

"But there are some negatives," Hashemi said. "In the process of delivering the malware, we'll more than likely lose the ability to turn the cameras on and off later."

"Can't we sneak back in like we did tonight and install another Pikachu?" Bradley asked.

Jackson was already shaking his head. "Guys, Kayla somehow hacked into the security cameras." He quickly laid out what he and Charlie had deduced moments before. "That's the only way they could have set this up," he concluded. "So no, we're not sneaking back in. At least, not like this."

"Sure, Kayla Hall could have installed another Pikachu in order to power on the cameras, but she does *not* have control of the security system," Megan said.

"Think about it," Jackson said. "How else could she monitor the cameras and reposition them to spy on us?"

"It's impossible," Megan said. "I don't care how much money or time she had. The KRX Supreme security system can't be hacked. Kayla's good, but she isn't *that* good."

"Maybe she didn't hack the system. Maybe she stole the password to it," Charlie said. "Rule of Engagement Number Eleven: Don't use a bazooka when a slingshot will do."

Jackson glanced at Charlie. "We really need to talk about those rules of yours."

"What?" Charlie shrugged. "Sure, maybe they're . . . inspired by your Code of Conduct, but they're more different than alike."

"Yeah. Sure." Jackson put his hand to his ear. "But Charlie's right about her stealing the password, Megan. We've stolen more difficult things."

Megan sighed. "Yeah . . . The NVR is secure, but a cell phone or Kelsey's laptop are a lot easier to crack. And if she got the password from one of them, it's a cakewalk to remotely log into the system — especially if you're using another NVR to tie into it."

Jackson checked the time again. "For now, let's focus on getting out of here. We'll come up with a new plan later."

"What about the masters?" Gaby asked, holding up the two key rings.

Jackson stretched his arm toward her. "I'll take those."

She moved the key rings behind her back. "Come on, Jackson. You can't make it from here to the security room and back to Mrs. Cooper's room in three minutes."

"Or four minutes." He smiled. "I'm fast."

"But I'm faster," Charlie said. "I should go. And if it wasn't for me —"

"You've paid back your debt," Gaby said. "I'm faster than you both, and I can run longer, and I'm in better shape." She took a step toward Jackson. "Equal risk," she said. "If I'm in, I'm in."

Jackson gazed at her, taking in her long brown hair, her eyes that looked so wide behind her glasses, and her beautiful, perfect, raw, chapped lips. "Okay," he finally said. "You're up."

RUNS IN THE **FAMILY**

Jackson switched off the microphone again, then walked over to Charlie. The crew had been ready for over fifteen minutes, yet Charlie kept pacing in front of the chalkboard, yanking and pulling his hair. Every few minutes he would stop, pull his own notebook from his back pocket to jot down an idea or two, then return to pacing.

"Time to go," Jackson said. "Samuel and Ray won't wait on us forever."

Charlie looked at the file cabinet holding the test. "Just give me a second. . . ."

"If you're hesitating because you're worried about Gaby, don't," Jackson said. "She can probably run to the security room, hook the key rings on the correct pegs, lock the door behind her, and stop by the vending machine for a soda all before the cameras power back on."

Charlie shook his head. "Gaby's not the problem. I've been thinking about your plan."

Jackson had overheard Charlie asking Bradley about

the original plan while they waited for Megan to prepare the malware program. He'd almost been embarrassed about it, it had so many holes. "Look, now's not the time to second-guess —"

"I'm not trying to criticize you," Charlie said. "It was a good plan, Jackson. It was just . . ."

"Just not good enough?"

Charlie shrugged. "At least you *had* a plan — using the two stationary cameras in the social studies wing to catch Rob and Thom breaking into Mrs. Clark's room. It had a few flaws, but it could have worked. Especially when you factor in the Sue Storm —"

"The Invisible Woman?"

"Yeah," Charlie said. "Because you were going to trick Rob and Thom into using *disappearing* ink during the test." He grinned. "It was pretty smart — and that would have stopped them from cheating."

"Maybe," Jackson said. "That was plan B. Did Bradley tell you about plan A?"

"With the tablets?"

"I'm surprised. No fancy nicknames?"

"Actually, Bradley's been calling them Han van Meegerens, after the Dutch forger who —"

"Let's just stick with 'tablets,'" Jackson said. "I canned that when Hash and Megan convinced me they could build the Pikachu. But now I'm wondering if we can make the original plan work again." He pulled his notebook from his jacket. "I just can't figure out how to sneak back in to turn off the cameras, much less set up the . . . Han van Meegerens. As long as Kayla has control over those cameras, there's no way we can anticipate what she'll do — when she'll turn then on, or reposition them, or anything."

"You know Megan's been working on a password-decoding program."

"We are not breaking into Kayla Hall's house."

"I know, I know," Charlie said as he flipped open his notebook. "But I think plan A could work. And with a few tweaks, we might even be able to catch whoever's behind this."

Jackson read Charlie's scrawled handwriting. Then he pulled the notebook out of Charlie's hands and read it a second time. "Are you insane?"

"Jackson, think outside the box."

"More like outside the universe." He handed the notebook back to Charlie. "But it *could* work."

"It *will* work. But we need a carrot to dangle in front of the roadrunner."

"I think you're mixing your metaphors, but I get what you mean." Jackson pocketed his notebook, then he and Charlie walked over to Gaby, who was running in place, warming up for her sprint to the security room. Jackson paused before lightly touching her shoulder. Was he supposed to talk to her differently now that she was officially his girlfriend?

"What is it, Jackson?" Gaby asked, still jogging.

Jackson realized that he'd been staring. "Oh, sorry. . . . I don't want you to put the keys back on the pegs," he said.

Gaby started stretching. "Don't worry about me running out of time. You know I can make it."

"It's not about that," he said. "Just place the keys on the table. And don't lock the door behind you. I want to —" He looked at Charlie. "*We* want to dangle a carrot in front of the roadrunner."

"That makes absolutely no sense."

"What can I say, it's Charliespeak." He winked. "Trust me. Okay?"

Gaby nodded. "Okay."

Jackson turned toward Bradley. "Are those molds dry?"

"Dry enough so they won't be damaged when we run."

"Good. Let's get into position." He turned on his microphone. "Megan, Hash — you guys ready?"

"We're ready," Hashemi said. "I just . . . I can't believe I'm doing this to the Pikachu."

"Hashemi, stop acting like that little slimy dude from *The Lord of the Rings*," Charlie said. "It's a machine. A machine you didn't even get out of beta."

"Exactly," he moaned. "And now I won't even be able to retrieve it to repurpose the parts."

"Buck up, Gollum. Thanks to Charlie, we might be able to figure out a way to get your machine back," Jackson said. "Megan, start the sequence. Everyone go on my mark." Then he leaned close to Gaby's ear. "Good luck," he whispered.

Gaby didn't look at him. In her head, she was already following the route she'd mapped out to the security room, reminding herself to avoid the patch of shoddy carpet in front of Mrs. Vick's classroom and the uneven bit of trim at the hallway door. Charlie had offered his earpiece so Megan could update her on the cameras, but she declined.

She didn't want the distraction of someone talking in her ear as she ran.

"Get ready," Jackson said behind her.

She wiped her hands on her pants, then repositioned her glasses. This would have been a great day to wear contacts.

"Megan has started the program," Jackson said. "It looks like it's working," he continued, his voice rising. "The cameras are blinking off. . . . And . . . go!"

Gaby flung the door open and shot down the hall, the two key rings tight in her hand. The metal cut into her palm, but that just made her run harder. In the atrium, she passed Megan, her long blond hair streaking behind her. A few seconds later, Hashemi lumbered past, the MATE tight in his grasp.

As Gaby neared the security room, she was glad to see that they had remembered to leave the door cracked. She rammed her shoulder into it, throwing it open, and staggered for a second before regaining her balance.

She dropped the keys on the desk and shot back out the door.

Her legs were beyond tired, but she didn't dare stop to rest, or wipe her forehead or palms, or brush her bangs from her face. She just kept running — through the atrium, down the hallway, and into Mrs. Cooper's classroom.

Jackson was waiting for her outside the window.

"What are you —"

"Stop talking. Keep moving," Jackson said as he helped her climb over the windowsill. "I'll close it," he yelled. "Just go!"

She took off, with Jackson following close behind. Finally, she reached the picnic tables and collapsed on the ground. She felt so dizzy, she thought she might throw up.

Megan glanced at her over her laptop. "The outside cameras are just turning on," she said. "You made it with thirty seconds to spare. Good job, Gaby."

Jackson nudged Charlie. "Told you . . . she'd have time . . . for a soda."

Charlie rolled his eyes as he helped Gaby to her feet. "Show-off," he said before hugging her and kissing her cheek.

Bradley grinned as he elbowed Jackson. "Maybe you should be taking notes."

PULLING BACK THE CURTAIN

On Saturday morning, after his parents left home to take Samuel to the airport, Jackson turned on his computer and inserted the flash drive. Hashemi and Megan had offered to review the video with him, but this was something he needed to do himself. Whoever was blackmailing them wouldn't make a careless, overt mistake — he or she was much too smart for that. Jackson was looking for small, subtle clues.

He reread the list that Gaby had created of all the potential suspects and added a few more names. And then, after a sip of Earl Grey, he got to work.

He figured it out by camera number four.

While most other students walked normally from class to class, Victor Cho kept his head low as he passed each camera. He was a master at minimizing his screen time, as if he knew exactly how each camera was oriented and where to walk to avoid them. He didn't talk to many people in view of a camera, and when he did, he covered his mouth. And although he never spoke to Rob and Thom, their expressions clearly indicated that they not only knew who Victor was, but that they answered to him.

In retrospect, Jackson thought, he should have immediately made Victor the number one suspect. Victor had more than enough money to pay off Eric Caan and Kayla Hall. He was certainly smart enough — he didn't win all those chess competitions with his looks — and he had no problem letting others know just how intelligent he was. And he had the motivation. Although Jackson had never publicly said anything about the Election Job, there were plenty of rumors floating around school about Victor's involvement, and how he had sold the team out to Keith. The Chess Team even kicked him out because of it.

Finally, Victor had been a part of the crew. He knew them better than anyone.

Jackson picked up his phone. A few rings later, Charlie answered.

"Are you looking for Gaby?" he asked. "She's not —"

"I'm calling for you," Jackson said. "How are you feeling?"

"Sore," Charlie said. "Just thinking about walking makes my legs hurt. And you?"

"Less sore. More mad," Jackson said. "How are those tweaks to the plan coming along?"

"Good, I think. Just need the name of our mastermind."

Jackson looked back at the image of Victor frozen on his screen. "Well, today's your lucky day."

CARLITO IN CHARGE

Gaby took in a deep, cold breath of air as she and Charlie walked toward Hashemi's house. Sunday had seemed to drag on forever — first mass, then a big lunch with her *tías*, and then hours of homework. But when four o'clock hit, their mother let them leave the house, as long as they promised to be back by dinner.

She rubbed her hands together. She hadn't seen Jackson since Friday night, and they had plenty to talk about, like that whole boyfriend/girlfriend conversation. But Jackson had been tied up all weekend with Charlie, working on "something big." The few times she emailed him, he refused to tell her what the plan was. All he would say was that Charlie would be running the crew. She thought that would have made Charlie giddy. Instead, he seemed to grow more and more pale the closer they got to Hashemi's.

They were the last to arrive at the shed. The others had already crowded around the worktable.

Charlie waved feebly. "Hey, guys."

"Finally," Megan said. She turned to Jackson. "Now will you explain what's going on? You've got a new plan, right?"

"*We've* got a new plan," he replied, nodding toward Charlie. "Charlie's going to walk us through it."

The shed seemed deathly quiet as Charlie and Gaby joined the others at the table. Charlie peeled off his coat, exposing his sweat-soaked T-shirt. Jackson raised his eyebrows at Gaby, but she just shrugged.

"Okay, guys, so, as you know, we ran into a few speed bumps on Friday night," Charlie began. He was looking at his notepad, but Gaby was pretty sure he wasn't reading it. The page was blank. "But like Jackson said, we have a plan."

"Please tell me we're going to get Victor too," Megan said.

Charlie nodded. "Absolutely. Well, probably. I mean, there are some challenges — nothing serious . . . A few rocks in the road . . . A boulder or two at most, but —"

"What Charlie is trying to say is that as long as Victor stays true to character, we're confident that we'll get all three of them," Jackson said.

Megan crossed her arms. "And what about Kayla the Cheat?"

"I think, given the circumstances, that Victor, Rob, and Thom are good enough," Jackson said.

"And Kayla's not really a bad guy," Hashemi said. "At least, *I* don't think so."

Megan leaned toward Jackson. "I've been thinking about Kayla's computer system . . ."

"Megan . . ." Jackson began.

"I'm not suggesting that we break into her house. Although, if we did, we could —"

"We'll discuss this later," Jackson said. "After the briefing."

"So what's the plan, Jackson?" Bradley asked. He shook his head. "I mean, Charlie."

Charlie flipped the page and focused on his notes. "First we're going to, um . . . meet with Victor. And then we're going to, um . . ."

"Since Victor and Kayla have a way to control the cameras, maybe you should start by explaining how we're going to deal with that threat," Jackson said.

"Yeah, um . . ." Charlie took a deep breath. "We have to, uh . . . even the odds. . . ." He licked his lips. "So we're going to . . . um . . ."

"Okay, let's take a quick time-out," Jackson said as he rose from the table. He led Charlie away from the group. "Dude, get a grip. Why are you so nervous?" he asked.

"I don't know," Charlie said. "What if things go wrong?"

"That's why we plan."

"But Victor almost caught us."

"But he didn't. And he won't." Jackson looked back at the group. "It's a good plan, Charlie. You have to believe that. Because if you don't, why would you expect them to?" He punched Charlie's shoulder. "Remember Rule Number Eight: Never let them see you sweat, even if it's ninety-nine degrees outside."

Charlie choked. "You read the de la Cruz Rules of Engagement?"

"Bradley emailed them to me yesterday. They're . . . *interesting*."

"They're still a work in progress —"

"They're in beta?" Jackson laughed. "Hash would love that." Then he stopped smiling. "Look, don't try to go up there and be me. Just be yourself," he said. "They're your crew, but they're also your friends. Just talk to them like you always do."

Charlie nodded. "Be myself. Okay. I can do that."

Jackson and Charlie rejoined the group. "Let's try this again," Charlie said, closing the notebook. "We're going to . . ." He paused as he stole a quick glance at Jackson. Jackson flashed him a thumbs-up. "We're going to pull an Isabel Lahiri with a Ben Kenobi, a Mutara Nebula, two Han van Meegerens, a Sue Storm, a White Elephant, a pair of Mr. Magoos, and a Super Bowl Forty-Seven."

No one spoke for a few seconds. Finally, Megan and Hash turned to each other. "I have no idea what any of that means," she said. "But at least he used a *Star Trek* reference."

Bradley leaned toward Gaby. "Did you know that Han van Meegeren was a famous Dutch painter and art forger?" He patted his chest. "Charlie got that from me."

"How many silent partners do you think we need?" Jackson asked.

"Two or three," Charlie said. "I've already talked to Carmen about the Environmental Action Team helping out."

"Are you sure?" Jackson asked. "It's one thing for them to place a few extra bins in the hallway. It's another to —"

"Trust me. I know people. They want to help."

"Fair enough. It's your call." Jackson slipped on his coat. "Once the crew has calmed down, you'll need to give them a little more explanation."

"Hey, since Charlie is in charge, maybe he's the one I should be talking to about Kayla," Megan said.

Charlie shrugged. "Megan does have a point —"

"Charlie!"

"Come on, Jackson. You know we could figure out a way to get Kayla as well."

Jackson glanced at the box of watches on the work-table. "We'll see."

"So where are you off to?" Bradley asked.

"I need to talk to Rob and Thom. . . . Tell them about our hiccups with breaking into the school." He picked up a screwdriver and shoved it into his pocket. "And then I have to deliver a message to Victor Cho."

UNANNOUNCED GUESTS

"Do you think he'll show up?" Charlie asked on Monday morning as he and Jackson stood in front of the toolshed in the school garden.

"He will if he wants his bike pedals back." Jackson blew on his hands. He'd figured a mile-long walk would be a good way to get Victor's attention. He just hoped it didn't make Victor too late.

Finally, at 7:31, they saw Victor walking his bike across the parking lot.

Jackson tapped his watch as Victor leaned his bike against the fence. "A minute late. I guess that's acceptable, given the circumstances."

"Want to tell me what this is about?" Victor asked. His glasses had fogged over. "Why are we even meeting here?"

"You should know better than anyone," Jackson said. "The security cameras aren't aimed this way. It's one of the only private locations on campus."

"That is, unless you told Kayla to reorient the camera this morning," Charlie said.

"I have no idea —"

"Don't," Jackson said. "You'll save us all a lot of time."

A smile spread across Victor's face, and his shoulders went back as he straightened his stance. It was almost like he transformed into someone else. Someone with more confidence. Swagger.

"Took you long enough," he said. "What tipped you off?"

"I saw the video of you dodging all the cameras," Jackson said. "The only way to avoid them as well as you did was to know exactly where they were pointed."

Victor rocked back and forth on his heels. "Smart. And I thought it would be Tweedledum and Tweedledee who spilled."

"So why did you do it?" Charlie asked.

"I have my reasons."

"You're a liar and a cheat," Charlie said.

"Takes one to know one."

"Look, I don't care why you did it," Jackson said. "But this is how it's going to work in the future. Even though you tried to trick us, we're going back in to get that test. Then you're going to hand over the hard drive and the doctored video."

Victor crossed his arms. He had expected Jackson to say a lot of things, but not that. "You're . . . actually going to sneak back in?"

"Yes," Jackson said. "And you're going to switch off the cameras for us."

"Maybe I should turn in the video right now. Save us all the hassle," Victor said as he adjusted his frames.

He didn't need to wear them — the lenses were just glass — but he liked how they made him look. "I've got a solid B-plus going into the final. I don't need the test answers."

"But Rob and Thom do," Charlie said. "They're not going to be too happy if they hear you're stopping us from sneaking in. That the whole idea of us stealing the test is a cover to catch Gang Greene on video."

Victor snorted. "What are they going to do? Squeal? If so, I'll show Dr. Kelsey the real video of Rob and Thom flooding the school." He grinned. "I've got all the angles covered."

Jackson knocked on the toolshed. "Hear that, boys?"

The shed door swung open. Rob and Thom stepped out, and Rob tossed the two bike pedals at Victor's feet. "You trying to double-cross us, Cho?"

Victor took a step back. "Don't you see what Jackson's doing? It's classic divide and conquer."

Thom shook his head. "So all this was really to catch them on video?"

"And what's wrong with that?" Victor asked. "Think about it — with a *real* video of them breaking into the school, we could force them to steal Mrs. Clark's exam and anything else you want. We could blackmail them until the end of the year."

"Believe what you want," Jackson said to Rob and Thom. "But remember, you guys aren't the first people who Victor tried to burn."

"But you burnt me first," Victor said. "It's an eye for an eye."

Jackson spun toward Victor. Victor hadn't been scared before, but he had also never seen Jackson angry. "You know, you've gone to a lot of effort and spent a lot of money just to get revenge," Jackson said. "But you have to realize we didn't do anything wrong during the Election Job. We didn't force you to switch sides."

"But you planned on it," Victor said. "You set me up to fail."

"Jackson," Charlie said softly as he placed his hand on Jackson's shoulder. "Maybe you should —"

"I'm okay," he said, shaking Charlie off. "I just want Victor to tell me how we set him up during the Election Job. How we tricked him."

"You . . . you forced Keith into —"

"Into what? Talking to you? Offering to spare the Chess Team if you flipped on us?" He shook his head. "No. We hoped you wouldn't turn, but if you did, we wanted to be prepared to capitalize on it." He flexed his hands. "We had contingencies in place if you hadn't sold us out. The plan would have worked either way."

"But you . . . you —"

Victor stopped talking as a car pulled into the parking lot. The boys all looked at the car, their eyes wide-open, as Valencia Bianchi and her sister, Serena, cruised past.

"We need to go," Jackson said. "The last thing we need is Serena coming out here to check on us. Or worse, telling Dr. Kelsey that she saw us." He frowned at Victor. "This is your fault for being late."

"Don't blame this on me," Victor said. "And I'm not worried about Serena. But then again, *I'm* not the one suspected of flooding the school." He picked up his bike pedals. "I promise not to try to record you again. But you'd better get us that test. If not, Kelsey gets the video." He walked to the gate but paused before opening it. "Time's ticking, Jackson. Get to it."

a DEAL WITH THE DEVIL

Usually when the last bell of the day rang, Serena remained in class a few extra minutes until the hallways emptied. But today she was the first person out of the room, bumping and elbowing the other students as she fought her way to the library.

Lincoln was waiting at the door. "You sure about this?"

"Positive," she said. "I told you — I saw them all in the garden. Jackson's up to something, and he's somehow got Victor, Rob, and Thom involved. Why else would they be meeting there that early in the morning?"

"Maybe they like flowers."

"I'm being serious," she said. "I also asked Mr. James if he noticed anything strange. Turns out, there are a couple of gaps in the videos from Friday night. It's like the security cameras switched off and on a few times. His master keys to the teachers' rooms were lying on his desk this morning, not on the pegboard like usual. And the security room door was unlocked."

"It's wintertime, Serena. The power always goes out in spurts in January."

"But what about the keys and the door?"

"This is Mr. James we're talking about, remember?"

"Okay, fine." She pulled a folded sheet of paper from her purse. "I called in a favor from one of the student helpers in the guidance office. All those guys have one teacher in common. Mrs. Clark. They must be planning to cheat on her semester exam."

"How do you know about the exam?" he asked, taking the printouts from her.

"My sister," she said. "It was the one class that she got a B in." Serena was probably the only student at Maplewood who hoped Mrs. Clark wouldn't retire after the school year. She wanted as many chances as she could get to one-up her sister.

Lincoln flipped through the schedules. "You got these from James Brightwell, didn't you?"

"What? He was happy to print out a few schedules —"

"In return for the Honor Board looking the other way when he 'accidentally' writes on the bathroom wall again?"

"I only told him I'd *consider* his helpfulness the next time he's in trouble," she said. "And police use informants all the time. Why can't we?"

"Um, because we're not the police." He passed the printouts back to her. "You really think this is about Mrs. Clark's exam?"

"It has to be. Remember how they were meeting in the newsroom last week? It's right down the hallway from Mrs. Clark's room. They were probably scoping out her classroom and the hallway. Trying to figure out a way past the cameras."

"Wait — you think they're going to *steal* the exam? Like, from her room?"

"I wouldn't put it past Jackson," Serena said. "Would you?"

Lincoln let out a long sigh. "If you really think that's what he's trying to do — and that's a big *if* — we have to go to Dr. Kelsey."

"No way. Dr. Kelsey could have ended this a long time ago if he'd just brought them before the Honor Board."

"He didn't have proof."

"That's why I'm going to get it for him," Serena said. "I didn't spend all those hours reviewing video just to let Dr. Kelsey swoop in and get all the glory. If Jackson's really going to steal Mrs. Clark's exam, I want to be the one to catch him."

And if I catch Jackson, I'll be a shoo-in for Honor Board chair next year.

Lincoln frowned at her, then opened the library door. "Okay. Let's go. He's already inside."

He and Serena crossed the library, then stopped at a table in the corner of the room. Keith Sinclair took a bite of his candy bar but didn't speak. He was sitting right below a sign that read NO EATING.

"Thanks for agreeing to meet," Lincoln said.

Keith took another bite of the candy bar. "Make it quick, Miller."

Lincoln and Serena sat down at the table. Last year, when Serena was a sixth grader, she had been enamored with Keith Sinclair. He was a starter on the basketball team and president of the Gamer Club. He seemed like such a leader. Some of her friends had even tried to flirt with him, though all that usually meant was that they went into giggle fits whenever he passed.

But that was a year ago. . . . Before the Student Council elections.

"We need your help," Lincoln began.

"You mean, like how you helped me during the election fiasco?" he asked. "No thanks."

Lincoln glanced at Serena, then started again. "The hard drive to the school security system was stolen a little over a week ago," he said. "Unfortunately, the school budget doesn't allow for a replacement."

"Why don't you get Gaby and the Student Council to buy one? They've already taken all the money from the Gamer Club."

Serena cleared her throat. "As I understand it, that's only because you didn't have enough members to constitute a real student organization."

Keith turned to Serena. "And who are you?"

"Serena Bianchi. Student Honor Board member. We're investigating the break-in and —"

"I don't care," he said. "Kelsey's got me working like a grunt, all because my dad won't give him any more money. You think I'm going to do something to make his life easier? Or yours?"

Serena leaned into the table. "With one small donation, you could be back in study hall, playing games on your phone like everyone else."

"There's no way my dad would ever agree to another contribution, not after all the money he . . . *donated* to Dr. Kelsey," Keith said.

Serena took a breath and reminded herself that what she was doing wasn't wrong. She wasn't breaking the rules. She was encouraging a fellow student to support the school. His motives didn't matter, and as long as hers were focused on justice, it was okay.

"A hard drive, while expensive, is certainly within your personal price range," she said.

He took another bite of his candy bar. "Are we finished here?"

"Think about it this way," Serena said. "There has to be one other person you dislike more than Dr. Kelsey. Or Gaby de la Cruz." She pulled out her keys and jingled them against the table. "Isn't there a reason they call it the Great *Greene* Heist?"

Keith's eyebrows twitched. "Jackson?"

"That's why we need the system. We want to catch him in the act of breaking into the school. We think he's trying to steal a test."

Keith wrapped his candy bar and placed it on the table. "Okay, Serena Bianchi. You've got my attention."

PREPARING FOR CHECKMATE

As Victor paused a few steps away from Kayla Hall's bedroom on Monday evening, he sniffed his clothes. He'd spent the afternoon playing chess at the nursing home, so he'd coated himself in his father's cologne to mask the stench of Bengay and disinfectant. He hated playing with the old-timers — they took too long to make a move and always wanted to talk about the "good old days" — but at least they provided better competition than the idiots he played against online.

Victor had tried to explain to the Chess Team that by abandoning Jackson's crew during the Great Greene Heist, he had played the odds. Made the correct, strategic move. Did what was best for the team. Unfortunately, no one else saw it that way. Although he wasn't officially kicked off the Chess Team, they kept rescheduling the meetings and forgetting to tell him about the new dates. And in the few meetings he did make, he spent most of the time sitting by himself while his "friends" opted to practice with snot-nosed sixth graders rather than him. Finally, he quit the team. Unlike his old teammates, the senior citizens didn't care that he turned on Jackson Greene. They just wanted to play chess . . . and talk.

Victor knocked on Kayla's open door, then entered her room. "Your mother let me in."

"I know." She nodded toward one of the monitors on her desk. The screen was split into four quadrants — video feeds of her porch, front yard, backyard, and the sidewalk.

"Is it even legal to record people walking on the sidewalk?"

"You're one to talk," Kayla said as she wrinkled her nose. Whatever cologne or deodorant he was wearing smelled overbearingly sweet — like cake doughnuts coated with sugar and butter and honey.

"Don't get too used to that system," Victor said, settling into a chair. "Come next week, I'll need all of that equipment back. I don't want to leave any loose ends."

"So you're going to just throw it away?" She stopped typing to glance at the NVR on her desk. "This system is practically brand-new."

"With all the cash I'm giving you, you can buy a new system if you want." He scooted his chair closer, and Kayla covered her nose. "But forget about that. I talked to Jackson and Charlie this morning. They're going to steal the test."

"Do you want me to try to catch them on video again?"

"Of course. That's the whole point of the Great Greene Payback," Victor said as he reached into his khakis, pulled out a pocket watch, and checked the time.

The watch was black and shiny and hipster-fake. Kayla stopped herself from rolling her eyes. Really, who even used a pocket watch anymore? If he was going to hassle with taking something out of his pocket whenever he wanted to check the time, he might as well use his phone.

Function over form. Some guys just didn't understand.

"Well, their electrical switch is toast," Kayla said. "They won't be able to turn off the cameras remotely. I suppose one of them could run through the hallways like they did last time, though we could reprogram the oscillating cameras to limit that. I also upgraded both our system and the security cameras with every potential virus patch. If Megan tries to shut us down again, we'll be ready."

"Awesome," he said. "Best case, we catch Jackson in the act of stealing the test. Worst case, we turn in the doctored video." He fumbled with his watch for a second before snapping it closed. "Either way, come the end of the week, Jackson Greene truly will be infamous."

FULL-COURT PRESS

On Tuesday afternoon, a few minutes after the final bell rang, Lynne Thurber leaned against the wall in the atrium. She was supposed to be in the gym, warming up for basketball practice, but she had a favor to pay out first.

She pushed herself off the wall as soon as the main office door swung open. Dr. Kelsey stepped into the atrium, right when Jackson said he would.

"Dr. Kelsey, do you have a few moments?" she asked, rushing to catch up with him. "I wanted to talk to you about Thursday's game against Riggins."

He almost seemed to speed up. "Make it quick, Ms. Thurber."

She was glad she had long legs — it took everything she had to keep up with him. "I wanted to know if you were coming to see us play. We could use all the support we can get."

"I'm sure you girls will do fine."

"This is our toughest matchup of the year. Riggins has only lost one game, and that was because half of their team was sick with the flu," she said. "They're all that stand between us and the top seed in the play-offs."

"Isn't that a bit presumptuous?" He pulled out a hand-kerchief and wiped his nose. "You're playing *at* Riggins while the boys are playing here, correct? As you know, I always attend the home games."

The boys' *home games*, Lynne wanted to say. "Our game might end up getting a lot of attention," Lynne said. "I'm friends with one of the girls from their team, and she says that a reporter from FOX28 might be there. Their coach has already invited Dr. Accord and the school board —"

"The superintendent is planning to attend your game?"

Lynne reminded herself to look nonchalant. "Yeah, I think so. My friend said they're giving him a tour of their gym. I think they've asked for new lockers — something about trying to use up some surplus funding." She shook her head. "Can you believe it? We might actually get on TV! We'll be famous."

Dr. Kelsey rounded the corner toward the security room. When he had contacted the superintendent last week about a replacement hard drive for the security system, all he had received was a tongue-lashing about the damaged floors. Of course, considering that Katie Accord had transferred from Maplewood to Riggins last summer, Dr. Kelsey shouldn't have been surprised that the superintendent had found extra room in his budget for his daughter's school.

Dr. Kelsey knocked on the security room's door. "Are you positive that Dr. Accord will be there?" he asked.

Lynne shrugged. "You could ask Coach Rainey. She'd probably know for sure what's happening."

He shook his head. It *would* be like Coach Rainey to keep this information from him. She had never gotten over him slashing her budget last year. He had even stopped asking her out — he figured he'd try again once the season ended.

Mr. James opened the door. "Hey, Dr. Kelsey." His smile widened once he noticed Lynne.

"Hi, Mr. James," Lynne said. "We've got an away game on Thursday. You'll see us off, right?"

He popped a sunflower seed into his mouth. "See you in the parking lot."

Lynne cocked her head. "You know, you should come to the game too, Mr. James. It'll be the best one of the year. Much better than —"

"Mr. James will need to remain at school, I'm afraid, but you can tell Coach Rainey that I'd be happy to attend," Dr. Kelsey said. He looked past her, and Lynne turned around to see Keith Sinclair and Serena Bianchi walking toward them. "If that's all, Ms. Thurber . . ." He gave her a small nudge. "See you on Thursday."

TIME IS NOT ON OUR SIDE

Bradley was the first person at the shed on Tuesday afternoon. He unlocked the door, flipped the light switch that Hashemi had reluctantly repaired, and got to work mixing paints, inks, and powders. Every few minutes, he would use the small tabletop ultraviolet lamp to check the legibility of the ink. The ink had to be strong enough to be read under faint UV light, but weak enough to be invisible in regular lighting. And, of course, it had to be completely formulated in two days.

Bradley's face and hands were covered in ink by the time Jackson and Charlie entered the shed an hour later. "You look like you got into a fight with a highlighter," Jackson said.

Bradley rubbed his forehead, getting even more fluorescent paint on his face. "This would be a lot easier with Megan's help."

"You know how Hash gets under pressure. We need her to work with him on the tablets." Jackson sat beside Bradley while Charlie settled down by the bundles of PVC pipe stacked against the wall. "Anyway, I thought all the Art Geeks mixed their own paint."

"Mr. Jonas won't let us anymore. Last time Lizzie tried, they had to fumigate the art room."

Jackson scooted his chair a little farther from the table. "Have you tried the ink with the watches?" he asked.

Bradley turned off the lamp, then pulled a watch from a nearby box. He pressed a button on the side, allowing a tiny ray of UV light to beam out of the watch casing. He held it close to the paper, and the ink lit up. "They'll have to write very lightly on their skin, but it should work."

"And how long will the ink last?"

"Two hours, I think." Bradley nodded toward a container of black ink. "Just about as long as disappearing ink lasts by itself."

"Good job," Jackson said. He took the watch from Bradley. "I can't believe Hash finally got something out of beta. On time."

"Technically, Megan took over working on the watches so Hashemi could finish the tablets."

Jackson dropped the watch back in the box, then noticed the UV dust clinging to his hand.

"Sorry," Bradley said. "That powder gets everywhere."

Jackson rubbed a few of the powder granules between his fingers. Then he reached over and turned on the lamp. The UV powder went from white to lime green.

"Can you grind this powder up any more?" Jackson asked.

"I think so."

"Good. The finer the better," Jackson said. "Let me know if you run into any issues." He crossed the room and knelt beside Charlie. "Do me a favor. When you get a chance, can you text —"

"Already done," Charlie said as he squinted at Hashemi's scrawled schematics for the two PVC stands. "She's on her way. So are Rob and Thom."

Jackson picked up a pipe. "I wonder how many times Hash designed these stands."

"He'd probably still be at it if the tablets didn't need more of his attention," Charlie said. "You two are a lot alike, you know. You're both insane planners."

"At least my projects get out of beta."

"And how's that plan to kiss Gaby coming along?"

Jackson grabbed a tape measure. "We are *not* having this conversation."

"Believe me, I don't want details. It's kind of gross, actually. I've smelled her breath in the morning."

"Charlie . . ."

"You know I'm making a killing by betting against you."

"Does everyone at school know that I haven't kissed Gaby yet?"

"No one but the crew. And the Environmental Action Team. And a few of the *Herald* reporters. And —"

"Charlie!"

He laughed. "All kidding aside, you really are a good planner." He looked at the PVC pipe in his hand. "Much better than me."

"You're good at it too. We came up with this plan together, remember?"

"I'm *okay* at it. And I'm getting better. But you're the best." He looked toward Bradley. "They deserve the best."

Jackson nodded a few times. "Thanks. We make a good team." Then he grinned. "Enough of the mushy stuff. Let's get to work."

Charlie read the schematics while Jackson cut the pieces for the two tripod bases for the tablet stands. They had just completed the first one when Rob and Thom entered the shed. "You're late," Jackson said.

"Yeah, and what are you going to do about it?" Rob replied. "What do you need us to do?"

"You mean, other than leave?" Jackson rose so he was eye level with Rob. "Grab a couple of the UV watches and some ink from Bradley. You need to practice writing lightly on your hand. It has to be light enough to —"

Jackson stopped as the shed door flung open. Megan ran to the group. "Guys. We have . . . a problem," she said between ragged breaths.

"Are you okay?" Jackson asked. "You sound like you ran all the way here."

"I did," she said. "It's about . . . the security . . . system."

Jackson eyed Rob and Thom. "Can this wait?"

She shook her head and sucked in a deep breath. "Can't. Running out . . . of time. . . ."

"Catch your breath," Jackson said. "Charlie, grab her a stool."

Rob crossed his arms. "What's she talking about?"

"Might as well tell them about the Mutara Nebula," Charlie said as he returned with a stool. "Victor and Kayla will find out when they try to log into the system."

"Okay." Jackson loosened his tie. "Keith Sinclair bought a new hard drive for the NVR."

"What? And you knew about this?" Rob asked.

"Knew about it?" Charlie grinned. "We planned it."

"It wasn't just bad luck that Serena saw us in the garden yesterday morning," Jackson said. "Serena's sister has been dropping her off early all year. We knew she was going to be passing by at that exact moment. We wanted to give her a little motivation to make sure she reached out to Keith about the hard drive."

Rob's brow furrowed. "You're telling me that you *wanted* the school to have a working security system?"

"No, but we didn't have much choice," Jackson said. "We thought it would be best if everyone operated on a level playing field."

"You're trying to trick us," Thom said.

"No, I'm evening the odds," Jackson said. "Now that the hard drive is being replaced, Mr. James and Dr. Kelsey will be able to use the NVR again. They can monitor everything from anywhere. So either we *all* avoid the cameras, or we all get caught." He turned to Megan. "Unless you've heard something new."

"No. Keith bought the hard drive, all right," she said, her breath now under control. "I called the security company again to verify it. The problem is, they're going to install it tomorrow morning. The appointment's during first period."

"What?" Jackson glanced at the PVC tripod base. "When we checked with the security company, they said the earliest they could be there was Thursday. We don't have enough time to finish the frames and sneak them in before the cameras go live tomorrow."

"Keith must have paid extra to have them move up the installation date," she said. "I talked to a few friends. He's not working for Kelsey anymore — he's already been moved back to study hall."

"Charlie, is there any way . . ."

Charlie was already shaking his head. "Even if we could get these frames finished today, there's no way to smuggle them in before first period. The Environmental Action Team won't be ready."

"I know Samuel's already back at college," Megan said. "But maybe we could cancel the school's installation appointment and Ray could pretend to —"

"There's no way we could afford an NVR hard drive, much less forge the security documents for him to fake being a technician." Jackson spun his pencil between his fingers. "We've got to sneak in tomorrow morning. It's then or not at all."

"Yeah, and 'not at all' isn't really an option." Charlie leaned against the table. "But I think we can make it work."

"Okay, you tell Gaby. I'll tell the others," Jackson said. "And look on the bright side, guys. Most plans have a major speed bump or two. We're just getting ours out of the way now."

SMARTER THAN THE AVERAGE CHEAT

The next morning, Jackson and Gaby held hands as they trailed behind the rest of Gang Greene on their way from the picnic tables to the school. Jackson had wanted to spend some alone time with her; her birthday was on Monday, and he was still hoping to get some ideas on how to upgrade her gift. But between planning for Operation To Catch a Cheat (as Charlie called it) and studying for Mrs. Clark's exam, he hadn't even had time to drop her an email, much less have a real conversation.

Unfortunately, Rob refused to give them any privacy at all.

"Let me get this straight," Rob said. "You don't think it'll look suspicious for all of us to walk into the newsroom this morning?"

"If anything, it'll help with our alibi when we do the same thing on Thursday afternoon," Jackson said. He turned to Gaby. "So like I was saying —"

"But Thom and I have never attended a meeting before."

"As long as you turn in those membership forms, you'll be fine. Charlie will take care of it if people start asking questions."

"You said Serena's been reviewing video for Mr. James, right? Maybe we can bribe her to unplug the cameras." Rob stopped walking, blocking Jackson and Gaby's path. "Me and Thom can be quite persuasive with the ladies."

Gaby gave Jackson's gloved hand a small squeeze. "I'm running ahead," she said. "Seems like you two have other things to talk about."

Rob waited until Gaby had caught up with the others before speaking again. "You're forcing us to take a big risk by going in during the basketball game." He looked around the virtually empty parking lot. "I mean, we're already here. Why don't we call Victor, tell him to turn off the cameras, and sneak into Clark's room now —"

"Trust me — Victor's not going to help us." Jackson rubbed his palms, trying to remember the feel of Gaby's hand in his. "Come on. Gaby's going to be late to her meeting if we don't hurry."

Rob fell into step beside Jackson. "You keep talking about sharing the risks, but Gaby sure does get off easy."

Jackson forced himself to keep walking. "She's got a basketball game, Rob. Think about it — how much attention would it draw if she was sitting in the stands with us at the boys' game instead of playing with the rest of the girls' team at Riggins? Anyway, she has her own role to play on Thursday afternoon."

They entered the school and followed the others to the social studies hall. Everyone stood just inside the doorway, underneath one of the security cameras.

"Okay, we don't have a lot of time," Jackson said, checking his watch. "Since *some* of us were late."

Thom shrugged. "I wanted to find the right shirt."

Charlie frowned at Thom's shiny gold-and-silver shirt. "Out of everything in your closet, that's what you chose to wear?"

"I wanted to stand out."

"You succeeded," Jackson said as he began unbuttoning his coat. "Don't forget, we have to look exactly like we'll look tomorrow. That means no coats and no bags." He turned to Hashemi. "Is the MATE ready?"

"Pulling up the camera app now," he said.

"Jackson!" Megan said. "Where are the recycling bins?"

Jackson looked down the hallway. "I thought the Environmental Action Team didn't rotate them out until tomorrow."

"They don't," Gaby said. "They must be cleaning the bins for us, since we'll be using them to sneak in the equipment on Thursday."

"I thought you were going to check with Carmen about this," Jackson said to Charlie. "Now what's Gaby supposed to stand on?"

"How was I supposed to know they were going to clean them out today?" Charlie ran his fingers through his hair. "Maybe we can drag a desk out of one of the rooms?"

"That'll draw way too much attention." Jackson tugged on his tie. "Options, people. We're running out of time."

"Someone needs to give Gaby a boost," Megan said. "That's the only way she can get high enough to record us at the right angle."

"Maybe she can climb on my shoulders," Bradley said.

Gaby took in Bradley's bony, wiry arms. He was a full head shorter than everyone else. "Thanks for the offer," she said, "but I think maybe we should pick someone taller."

"Hashemi's the tallest of us," Charlie said. "Maybe he can give her a boost."

"Wait," Thom said. "If Gaby is on Hashemi's shoulders, then he won't be in the video, right?"

Jackson paused. Thom was the last person he expected to figure that out.

"That's correct," Jackson finally said. "We'll be down another member." He looked down the hallway, toward the newsroom. "Megan, can you handle tech support on your own on Thursday?"

She shook her head. "I need Hashemi. I can't work all the programs by myself. We'll also want him nearby in case we have problems with the MATEs."

Jackson surveyed each member of the crew. "Okay, we can't lose Hash and Megan, and Bradley's too short." He narrowed his eyes at Rob. "You're the next tallest, Rob. You should be the one to give Gaby a boost."

"So I'll be sneaking into Mrs. Clark's room by myself on Thursday?" Thom asked.

"I'll go with you," Jackson said. "Charlie will take my place manning the first tablet stand."

"You guys must think I'm stupid," Rob said, his voice cutting through the hallway. He leaned against the brick wall and crossed his arms. "Victor warned us about something like this."

"What are you talking about?" Jackson rubbed his temples. "Come on, we don't have time for —"

"This is another trick," Rob said. "Another way to get me out of seeing the test myself."

"Thom will be there," Megan said. "Isn't one of you good enough?"

"You think I'd trust Jackson and Thom paired together? No offense, Thom." Rob nodded toward Charlie. "Let de la Cruz give his sister a boost."

Jackson allowed a small smile to slowly spread to his face. "One point for Rob. You're smarter than you look," he said. "Okay, guys, plan C. Charlie, you're up."

As the others peeled off their coats and book bags, Gaby placed her hand on Jackson's shoulder. "It was a good idea," she said.

"Not good enough." He glanced at Rob, who was staring them down.

"He really is smarter than he looks," she said, dropping her voice lower so only Jackson could hear her. "Be careful tomorrow."

He winked. "The basketball game is tomorrow and the test is on Friday. What else could go wrong between now and then?"

FeeLING SECURE

Serena stood up as the service technician from KRX entered the main office building during first period on Wednesday morning. "Please sign in," she said, pointing to the register on the counter. "Then I'll walk you to the security room."

She looked at the two administrative assistants behind the counter. She figured that they had seen her talking with Dr. Kelsey enough not to question her hall pass, but she still knew that the quicker she left the office, the better.

It had been easy enough getting a pass from Mrs. Kau in order to attend the KRX Supreme hard drive installation. Of course, she had yet to get approval from Dr. Kelsey or Mr. James. She figured in this instance it was best to act first and ask for forgiveness later. Worst case, they could always send her back to study hall.

But the way she saw it, they *owed* her. If it wasn't for her convincing Keith to make the donation, they wouldn't even have a new NVR hard drive.

Serena didn't speak to the tech as they headed to the security room, but she did keep sneaking sideways glances at him. He only looked eighteen or nineteen. Too young to be a "security expert."

She stopped in front of the door but didn't knock. "Don't take this the wrong way, but can you show me some ID?"

"Excuse me?"

The door swung open. "I thought I heard voices out here," Mr. James said. Then he frowned. "Serena, what are you —"

"I happened to be in the office, and I figured I'd walk the technician down here," she said. *Not technically a lie.*

Dr. Kelsey rose from the desk. "Shouldn't you be in class?"

"I'm only missing study hall," she replied. "Don't you think it might be good to have someone in here who's familiar with the machine? You know, since I spent *so much time* looking through all that video for you?"

Dr. Kelsey sighed. "Come on in. It's tight, but there's enough room for us all."

The technician moved toward the door, but Serena stepped in front of him. "We still need to see your badge, please."

The tech looked at Mr. James. "Sir, I —"

"I'm just trying to be careful," Serena said. "If he's who he says he is, showing ID shouldn't be a problem."

Mr. James pulled a packet of sunflower seeds from his shirt pocket. "Do what she says, son. It'll save us all a lot of time."

"Fine. Hold this," the technician said, shoving the box into Serena's hands. He opened his wallet and showed them all his KRX security card.

"Franklin W. Duke," she said, reading the card. "And what about a driver's license?"

"Look, little lady —"

"What's the problem?" Dr. Kelsey asked, now at the door. "You drove to the school, correct? I'm sure you're not operating a vehicle without a license."

The technician huffed but pulled out his license, which indeed read *Franklin W. Duke*. "Want a pint of blood as well?"

"No, this will be sufficient. Thank you." Serena stepped back to allow him to enter the room, then followed him inside.

Franklin looked around the small office. "This is your security room? Looks like a graveyard for electronics."

"How about you focus on the security system," Dr. Kelsey said.

The tech shrugged before sitting at the desk and picking up the NVR. "Since the cameras are already attached, this should be as easy as popping in the hard drive, recalibrating the system, and resetting the password, though some of the advanced features won't be operational until I upload all the data to the mainframe in the office."

"Once you reset the system, it'll be as good as new? And impossible to hack?" Serena asked.

"Well, virtually impossible," he said. "No system is completely secure."

She crossed her arms. "That's not what your advertising says."

He pulled a thick rectangular tablet from his bag. "I'll run a diagnostic to see if there are any other networks physically tied to the cameras. That would be the only way anyone could theoretically hack the system." He plugged a few of the camera cables into the tablet. "Looks like there are a few switches connected, but . . ." He squinted at the screen, then shook his head. "Nope, they aren't tied to an outside network. Or worst case, they're tied to a network that isn't powered on." He pressed a few buttons on the machine. "In my professional opinion, someone probably just did a sloppy job of running the wires. Did we do the Ethernet install for you guys?"

Dr. Kelsey fiddled with a button on his jacket. "Um . . . We went with a different service. You all were . . . outside of our price range."

Franklin unplugged the cameras from the tablet. "I can take a look if you'd like. Want me to work up a quote?"

Serena nodded. "Yes, thank you —"

"That's not necessary," Dr. Kelsey said. "You mentioned that you would reset the password, correct? I assume that would fix any potential issues."

"Yep. No way anyone else can tie into the system without the password. In addition, today's install comes with a free thirty-day trial of our Insta-Alert service. If anyone tries to hack your system or log in with an incorrect password, we'll immediately trace the signal back to its source."

"And will I still be able to view the cameras on my cell phone?" Dr. Kelsey asked.

Franklin was already pulling tools from his bag. "Anytime you introduce outside components to the KRX Supreme, you increase the risk of a security breach. You would be better off purchasing a few of our handheld monitoring devices. They're designed to be as secure as the KRX. If you buy three, you get a ten percent discount."

"I'm well aware of those options," Dr. Kelsey said. "Mobile access will be sufficient. I've already spent the money on new phones for me and Mr. James."

"Are your phones password-protected?" Franklin asked. After Dr. Kelsey and Mr. James nodded, he said, "Good. The network video recorder requires a twelve-character code for security reasons — a mix of letters, numbers, and symbols. You're not going to want to type that into the app every time you want to view the cameras. But as long as your phone has a system to lock the screen, the app will allow you to save the password."

Serena cleared her throat. "Maybe you should reconsider the handheld monitoring devices, Dr. Kelsey. We don't want any breaches."

"We're adults, Ms. Bianchi. We're more than capable of holding on to our phones. Isn't that correct, Mr. James?"

The security guard nodded. "Yes, Dr. Kelsey. Absolutely correct." He tugged at his collar. "Though mistakes do happen. We can't watch our phones twenty-four hours a day."

"Well, like I said before, I'm happy to continue monitoring the video cameras for you," Serena said. "In the morning and the afternoon — whenever you need me —"

"I appreciate the offer, but that shouldn't be necessary," Dr. Kelsey said. "With the new hard drive, reviewing the footage becomes much more manageable."

"But . . . Like the technician said, the system won't be fully operational for a while. What if we miss something today? Or even tomorrow?"

Dr. Kelsey crossed his arms. "Have you heard something?"

She quickly shook her head. "It's just . . . You can never be too sure. If something happens — and I'm not saying that it will, but it could — we should be ready. And it *is* a new system. There could be bugs."

"There aren't any bugs," Franklin said. "Though if you're worried about glitches or user errors, you can upgrade to our —"

"Just the installation, please." Dr. Kelsey said. Then he turned to Mr. James. "Since I'll be out for the next two afternoons, why don't you have Ms. Bianchi assist you with monitoring the cameras?"

"You're gone both days?" Mr. James asked.

He nodded. "Dentist appointment today. And don't forget, I got suckered into attending the girls' game at Riggins on Thursday."

Mr. James cleared his throat. "Sir, while I appreciate Serena's help, I'm more than capable of handling the security on my own."

"I understand. But you have to admit, it doesn't hurt to have an extra set of eyes."

"Of course," Mr. James said. He sighed. "I'd be . . . *happy* to have Serena's assistance."

Dr. Kelsey slapped Mr. James on the shoulder. "Good. We're all in agreement." He checked his watch. "Now, Ms. Bianchi, you should get back to class."

Serena had to fight to stifle her smile as she left the room. This was perfect. Mrs. Clark's test was on Friday. If Jackson was going to steal that exam, it would have to happen today or tomorrow. And now, she had the best opportunity to catch him in the act.

She still wished Dr. Kelsey had splurged on those handheld monitoring devices. Then she could keep track of Jackson all the time. But maybe Dr. Kelsey would order one for her next year . . . once she was chair of the Honor Board.

THE MUTARA NEBULA

Victor, Rob, and Thom sat on the couch in Kayla's bedroom on Wednesday afternoon. Rob's and Thom's elbows kept jutting into Victor's ribs, but he was too busy staring at the blank computer monitor to care. "Are you sure you can't log into the system?" he asked for the third time that afternoon. "Can't you at least try to —"

"Are you crazy?" Kayla asked. "This is the KRX Supreme we're talking about. Didn't you read the manual?"

They all shook their heads.

She picked up a thick booklet. "As soon as I try to hook back up to the network, the NVR will ask for a password. If I don't supply it within one minute, the Insta-Alert program will send a message to the system administrator and automatically trace the signal back here." She looked at Victor. "It's possible your school didn't splurge on the Insta-Alert — the price is outrageous — but I'm not about to take that chance."

Rob scooted forward, jutting Victor in the ribs again. "Maybe they didn't change the password. Maybe our old password works."

"Again, read the manual," Kayla said. "Of course they changed the password. It's standard protocol." She took off her glasses and placed them on the desk. "If you guys were able to get your hands on the security guard's cell phone, I could probably bypass the phone's PIN and get the password like last time. But there's no way I can access the KRX Supreme without it," she said. "That system is hack-proof."

Victor tried to remain calm. It had taken weeks of planning and watching Mr. James — mapping his napping schedule and security routine — in order for them to figure out the best time to steal his phone. After that, it took Kayla's program a full weekend to crack his phone PIN. They didn't have that kind of time.

He cleared his throat. "So you're telling me that without the password, we're totally blind?"

"Yes, but so is Jackson." She leaned back in her chair. "They're right, it really is like the Mutara Nebula." When no one responded, she continued, "You know, from *Star Trek II: The Wrath of Khan*. Only the best *Trek* movie ever."

Victor turned to Rob. "I thought you were supposed to be attending all of Jackson's meetings. How is it that you didn't find this out before yesterday?"

Rob shrugged. "And if you had known, what would you have done about it?"

"I would have talked to Keith. Convinced him not to pay for that new hard drive." Victor stood up from the couch. "But it doesn't matter. We still have the doctored video of Jackson's crew." He picked up his book bag and pulled a small box from it. "I need another favor," he said to Kayla. He handed her the box and waited for her to open it. "Those are the watches we're supposed to use on Friday. They put out UV light, allowing us to see the answers written on the back of our hands."

She held up one of the watches. "Slick. A little bulky, though." She pressed the button, letting out a small beam of light. "Looks like it works. What's the problem?"

"The problem is, I don't trust Jackson Greene. The battery will fail, or it'll blow up or something — there's no way he's going to let us walk into that exam with the answers."

Kayla studied a port on the side of the watch face, then began looking through her drawers. She finally pulled out a small cable. "If Megan and Hashemi have hidden something in there, I'll find it," she said. "But just to be clear, this will cost extra."

Victor grunted as he pulled his wallet from his back pocket. "And you say the Insta-Alert is overpriced. . . ."

THE **PALM** STING

On Thursday afternoon, Mr. James zipped around the school in his golf cart and sped toward the back of the building. In the fourteen years that he'd been working at Maplewood, it had become a tradition for him to see off the athletic teams when they had away games. And even though he was supposed to be monitoring the front exits, there was no way he was going to tempt fate by skipping the send-off. This game was too important.

"Glad you're still here. I was worried that I'd miss you," he said to Coach Rainey as he pulled up between her and the yellow school bus. The girls' basketball team was already streaming out of the gym, their shoulders weighed down with bags and other equipment. "Dr. Kelsey should be on his way to Riggins by now."

"Don't remind me," she said. "Honestly, I have no idea why he thinks the superintendent will be there. I would ask him, but that would require talking to him."

Mr. James had always liked Coach Rainey. They had started on the same day fourteen years ago. Her, a baby-faced recent college graduate. Him, a seasoned mall security guard working on a second career. He stepped out of his golf cart. "Are the girls ready?"

"They've been excited about this game all season. Especially Gaby." She looked at her watch. "Okay, let's load up." She gave Mr. James a high five, then stepped on the bus.

While a few girls waved at Mr. James as they passed by, Lynne Thurber and Gaby de la Cruz stopped right in front of him. "What do you think, Mr. James?" Lynne said. "Maybe if we win the championship, they'll finally upgrade our uniforms and gym bags."

"I'm sure Dr. Kelsey will keep that under advisement," he said.

She dropped her shoulder bag, creating a small dust storm. "Sorry about that," Lynne said. "I spilled a container of talcum all over me and Gaby's stuff. I thought I got it all off. I guess not." Lynne patted down her warm-up jacket, covering her hands in even more powder. "Where's my . . . Oh, never mind. It's not important." Then she high-fived Mr. James. "Sorry," she said as he waved powder away from his face.

Before he could respond, Gaby slapped his hand twice, hard enough to make his palm sting. She seemed to be covered in just as much talcum as Lynne.

"Wow, that stuff really gets all over the place," he said.

"Yeah, it's really clingy. I guess we didn't —" Gaby stopped and cocked her head. "Is that your phone?"

He frowned. "No, I don't think so. . . ."

"I heard it too," Lynne said. "Are you sure?"

He unclipped his phone from his belt and glanced at it. "No calls."

"I swore I heard something," Gaby said. "Maybe it was a text message or an alert of some kind."

Mr. James squinted at the phone as he pecked in his password with his index finger. Then he maneuvered the trackball to open first his text messages, then the security app. "No messages. No alerts." He returned the phone to his belt clip.

"I guess I must be hearing things," Lynne said. She turned to Gaby. "Where's Charlie?"

"I don't know," Gaby said. "Maybe he forgot —"

"He has to come!" Lynne said. "He's supposed to hug you before the game. It's tradition."

"Since when?" Mr. James pulled some sunflower seeds from the packet in his pocket. Jackson had seen the bus off more than Charlie had this season.

"It's . . . a new tradition," Gaby said. She looked around, and her gaze settled on Mr. James. "Um . . . Since he's not here . . . Mr. James, I hope it's okay if I . . ."

She was already moving toward him, her arms open to give him a hug. He found himself returning it. "Knock 'em dead, Gaby," he said.

She pulled back and stuffed her hands in her pockets. "Thanks. I guess I'm a bit more worried than —"

"There you are," Charlie said as he ran from the gym toward the bus with something white in his hand. "I thought y'all were boarding in the front of the school."

Why would he think that? Mr. James wondered. They always loaded up outside the gym.

Gaby met him halfway between the gym and the bus. Just as she reached him, Lynne yelled, "Ouch!"

Mr. James whipped his head toward her. "What's wrong?"

Lynne rubbed her arm. "I think . . . I think I got bit by a mosquito or something."

"In January? While you're wearing a jacket and a turtleneck?"

She shrugged. "My mom says I have sweet blood."

The bus driver honked the horn. "Hurry up, ladies!" Coach Rainey yelled. "We've got a game to play."

Gaby dusted off her hands as she rushed back toward Lynne and Mr. James. "Everything okay?" Lynne asked.

Gaby grinned. "Yep. Let's play ball."

BREAKING THE CODE

The rest of the crew was already huddled around a laptop when Charlie entered the newsroom. "Got it?" Jackson asked once the door closed behind him.

Charlie nodded. "Mr. James just started his security detail," he said. "My guess is, we've got at least twenty minutes."

"Good," Jackson said. They had been watching Mr. James enough to know that he never used his phone while cruising around on his golf cart. "Can you hit the lights while you're up?"

"But what about my program?" Megan asked. "Just let me try it. I'm sure I can hack the phone in a couple of hours. Certainly faster than Kayla the Cheat."

"Megan, that's great initiative, but we don't have two hours," Jackson said. "Bradley, grab that lamp from the box behind you."

Megan crossed her arms. "But —"

"Come on, Megan," Charlie said, sliding into the seat beside her. "You're starting to sound like Hashemi."

"You mean smart and passionate about technology?" Hashemi asked.

"Um, yeah. Exactly." Charlie handed Mr. James's phone, wrapped in a white handkerchief, to Bradley. "Let's hope this powder works."

"Are you sure you don't want to at least try the program?" Megan asked, still looking at her laptop. "We don't want to wear down the battery in the lamp."

"Megan, I promise, we'll use the program if this doesn't work," Jackson said. "Now, Bradley, if you don't mind . . ."

Bradley unwrapped the phone, then slid it underneath the UV lamplight. Four heavy lime-green fingerprints illuminated the keyboard.

"Four numbers," Megan said. "That's . . . twenty-four possible permutations. My program should be able to blow through that in three minutes."

Hashemi scooted a little to the left, outside of Megan's reach, then said, "Or maybe we can try the numbers in order of heaviest fingerprint to lightest." He pointed to the phone. "The order that Mr. James entered the PIN is fairly obvious."

She narrowed her eyes at Hashemi. *"Bruchon."*

"I'm not a traitor," he said, pushing his glasses to his face. "And for your information, the battery in the lamp works just fine. It's even strong enough to power a pneumatic battering ram."

Bradley punched in the numbers. "Code accepted. I'll pull up the security app." He read out the password to the KRX Supreme while Megan and Hashemi typed it into their respective laptop and tablet.

"The MATE accepted the password," Hashemi said.

"Same for me," Megan said. "We're in."

"Perfect," Jackson said. "Bradley, lights."

While Bradley went to flip back on the lights, Charlie leaned over Megan's shoulder. "Can you access the cameras?" he asked. "Just remember, don't reposition them. If Dr. Kelsey is watching the video, he'll know if you move —"

"Charlie, stop talking to me like I'm an idiot," Megan said as she typed. A few seconds later, she said, "Serena's sitting outside the security room."

"And Rob and Thom?" Jackson asked.

"Already in the gym."

"The Environmental Action Team will be moving those recycling bins into position in a few minutes." Jackson switched off the lamp and placed it in the box. "You ready, Charlie?"

"How is it that I always get to be the one stuck in confined spaces?" Charlie stood and stretched. "The Pikachu better be as easy to remove as you said. I'm not going to have a lot of time."

"It'll work." Jackson wiped down Mr. James's phone, then handed it to Bradley. "Okay, you guys know the drill. Personal cell phones, pencils, wallets — store everything that isn't essential in your book bag. Megan, text Rob and Thom and make sure they do the same. The last thing we need is someone's cell phone skidding across the floor as we sprint through the atrium."

Hashemi frowned. "Wait. What's this about sprinting?"

SERENA Takes Command

Serena was sitting outside of the security room, trying not to stare at the time on her flip phone, when Mr. James finally entered the hallway. As she jumped to her feet, he said, "I'm sorry I'm late. I got a little behind schedule at the gym."

"It's okay," she said, although she didn't mean it.

He pulled his keys from his pocket. "Next time, give me a call and I'll shoot right over."

She waved her phone. "I did."

He unlocked the door. "Hm . . . That's funny. The girls said they thought my phone had rung. They said —" He stopped as his hand fumbled around the empty belt clip. "I'll be . . . It seems that I've lost my phone."

"When do you last remember using it?"

"Maybe twenty or twenty-five minutes ago. I was talking with Gaby and Lynne," he said. "And then Charlie walked up and gave Gaby a hug and —"

"Mr. James! They stole your phone!"

"Nonsense. I would have noticed something like that."

She was already shaking her head. "We should find Charlie. Search and interrogate him. I bet he still has the phone on him. Or do you know Coach Rainey's phone number? Maybe Gaby took it with her."

He placed his hand on her shoulder. "Or maybe we should retrace my steps and make sure I didn't drop it in the parking lot."

They drove back to the gym, which was already beginning to fill with students and parents. Even though the best game of the day was happening a few miles away at Riggins, there were still a few people interested in seeing the Maplewood Middle School boys' team. Or rather, interested in seeing Riggins destroy the Maplewood Middle School boys' team.

After Serena called Mr. James's cell phone, they found it tucked underneath a juniper bush next to the sidewalk leading to the gym. Mr. James picked it up and inspected it. "Must have dropped it and somehow kicked it underneath this shrub." He tapped his temple. "First rule of being a good detective — always check the easiest solution first."

"That's . . . convenient," Serena said. She stepped off the sidewalk to allow a few parents to pass. "Please be careful with that phone, Mr. James. You can't trust anyone." She looked toward the gym, and for a second, she thought she saw Bradley Boardman standing in the doorway. But then a swarm of people entered the building, and he was gone.

"Don't worry," he said. "I'd better swing through the parking lot. Almost game time."

"Why don't you give me the keys? I'll head back to the security room."

"I thought you said I couldn't trust anyone," he said, a smile on his face.

"Mr. James . . ."

"Just kidding." He dropped the keys into her palm. "Sure you don't want a ride back to the other side of the building?"

"No thanks. I want to check something first."

She entered the gym, pushed past a few students, then flattened herself against the wall. Sure enough, Bradley sat in the stands, along with Jackson, Hashemi, Megan, Rob, and Thom.

But where was Charlie? And why wasn't Victor with them? Maybe he wasn't involved after all.

She quickly called Mr. James. "Is Charlie out there?" she asked after he answered the phone.

"Nope, don't see him."

"You're sure?"

He chuckled. "I may be getting up in age, but I can remember what Charlie de la Cruz looks like."

"Of course. Well, if you see him, can you let me know? Same with Victor Cho."

"I'm pretty sure I saw Victor biking off after school. But I'll call you if I see either of them."

Serena returned to the security room. Once inside, she dropped the keys on the desk and settled into the worn seat, trying to find a position that didn't hurt her back. The leather was hard and cracked, and tufts of white stuffing peppered the armrests.

After pulling up all the active cameras, she rotated the camera in the gym, centering it on Jackson's crew. She looked through a few other camera feeds, but she didn't see Charlie anywhere else in the building. Based on what Mr. James said, she knew he had been here after school. Either he'd left or he was out of view. Or maybe he was in Mrs. Clark's room.

She quickly reviewed the video from the camera outside the newsroom, then did the same for the camera centered on Mrs. Clark's door. Nothing out of the ordinary.

She spent most of the first half of the basketball game staring at Jackson on the computer screen, taking minimal note of everything else going on in the school. Most of the teachers had left, and the few who remained were either watching Maplewood get blown out by Riggins or serving on monitor duty. Other than a few members of the Environmental Action Team wheeling recycling bins down the hallways, the main building was empty. Students weren't usually allowed in the school halls during a basketball game — not unless they had a pass, like the Environmental Action Team.

Or unless they were members of the *Maplewood Herald* staff.

About a minute before halftime, Jackson and his crew rose from their seats. They each flashed a pass at Mr. Gonzales and entered the atrium. They seemed to be walking slowly, joking and laughing with each step. The whole group stopped in the middle of the atrium, laughing so hard that Bradley doubled over.

Serena leaned forward and tried to zoom the camera as close in on them as possible.

Then the screen went dead.

HURRY UP and WAIT

"Lights out!" Although Charlie was whispering, his voice rang load and clear through everyone's earpieces. "Move!"

Jackson and the crew took off toward the social studies wing. Charlie had rebooted the cameras, and they had forty-five seconds at most before they powered back on. Jackson could only hope that Serena wouldn't decide to come looking for them.

Jackson slid to a stop at the recycling bin underneath the camera pointing toward the newsroom. Bradley ran past him toward the bin outside of Mrs. Clark's room.

"What do you want me and Thom to do?" Rob asked.

Jackson yanked open the bin and pulled out a PVC tripod base and a telescoping PVC stand with a MATE mounted on top. "Shut up, sit in the newsroom, and stay out of the way." His watch beeped. Thirty seconds left. "Megan, I need to know the instant those cameras are up."

"Copy that," she said as she ran into the newsroom. A few seconds later, she said, "Just got a text from Samuel. He's in his dorm room and ready to make the call."

Jackson looked down the hallway. "Bradley — update!"

"Getting there!" Bradley was having a little trouble breathing, but he didn't dare stop to rest. He dropped to the ground, turned on his UV watch, then lined up his PVC tripod base with the fluorescent marks that Hashemi had made earlier that day. Once he was sure it was oriented correctly, he slid the telescoping PVC stand into the base and extended it to its full eight feet. The MATE attached to the top of the pipe wobbled for a few seconds before settling into place. The security camera now pointed directly at the tablet.

Bradley looked up and saw that Jackson had also completed his frame, blocking the other camera with an identical MATE. He flashed Jackson a thumbs-up.

"Hash! Megan! We're up," Jackson said, still kneeling on the floor.

"Cueing the video playback now," Hashemi replied.

"Outside cameras are restarting," Megan said.

Jackson checked his watch. "Five seconds . . ."

"And . . . we're live," Megan said.

"Starting the video now," Hashemi added.

Jackson crawled to the doorway to the newsroom, then leaned against the doorjamb. "And now, we wait."

SURVEYING THE DAMAGE

Serena spent the first few seconds after the cameras went dead tapping the keyboard. Then she checked the cables. The connection from the computer screen to the NVR looked solid, as did the connection from the cameras to the NVR. All the NVR lights were on, so whatever the problem was, it seemed to be with the cameras.

She was still fiddling with the cables when the screen came back to life. First the outside cameras powered on, followed by the ones inside the school. The resolution on some of the cameras wasn't as sharp as before — a few looked blue-tinted — but at least they were up and running.

Then she watched as Jackson's crew came onto the screen. They still seemed to be laughing as they filed into the newsroom and closed the door behind them.

She checked her watch. How many seconds had passed? Thirty? Forty-five? That wasn't enough time for them to sneak into Mrs. Clark's room and steal the test, was it? Or maybe they snuck into the main office instead — she was sure that the administrative assistants had copies of all the end-of-semester exams.

She rose from her chair. Maybe she should check things out, just to be on the safe side. Maybe —

The old black corded phone on the desk rang.

Serena stared at the phone for a few seconds, each ring seemingly sharper than the one before it. She didn't recognize the phone number on the display or its 215 area code, but she picked it up anyway.

"Hello, this is Alex from the KRX Call Center. May I speak with Mr. Josephat James?"

Josephat? What kind of name is that? Serena wondered. "I'm sorry, but he isn't here."

"Then may I speak with Eugene Kelsey?"

"Also not here."

"Hm . . . I see." There was the clacking of a keyboard on the other end of the phone. "And I'm speaking to whom?"

Serena gave him her name.

"Serena. Pretty name." He paused. "I don't see your name on the account. . . ."

"I'm a student," she said, winding the cord around her fingers. "Are you calling about the security system? Is something wrong?"

"Nothing to worry about. We just had to reboot the NVR and the cameras when we uploaded the new password to the mainframe."

"I thought that was supposed to happen yesterday."

"Sorry — we got backed up," he replied. "Are you monitoring the system now? Does everything seem to be running correctly?"

She looked at the screen. "Some of the cameras seem to have a different hue. And a few look a bit pixelated."

"I'd be happy to run a diagnostic," he said. "However, I'll have to take the cameras off-line again —"

"No, don't do that," she said. "It's fine." She paused for a second, then asked, "Since I've got you on the phone, can you see if anyone else is logged onto the system?"

"Sure," the tech said, with more clicks in the background. "Can you provide your login and passcode?"

Serena coughed. "I don't know . . . I don't have access to . . ."

"I'm sorry," he replied. "We take security very seriously at KRX. I can't run any checks on the system without proper verification."

That's actually pretty smart, she thought. "That's okay," she said. "Could you leave your name and phone number? I'll have Mr. James call you back."

He stated his name — Alex Westing — and gave her his phone number. It was the same number that had popped up on the display. Then he rattled off two more series of numbers — his ID and the case number for the call.

"Anything else I can help you with?" he asked.

Serena settled into the chair. "No thank you," she said.

"Well, if you don't mind, would you consider taking a survey to rate our service?"

"I don't think —"

"We'll throw in a free sixty-day trial of one of our handheld monitoring devices."

Serena leaned back. "There must be a catch."

"No catch. If you don't like the device, just return it before the end of the trial period. We won't bill you until afterward."

Serena figured she probably didn't have the authority to take the survey. But she wanted that device.

"How long will it take?" she asked.

"Ten minutes, tops," he said.

"That long?"

"They make you work for it," he said. "So come on. What do you say?"

She looked at the clock ticking away in the corner of the computer monitor. Ten minutes for a handheld monitoring device? That was a deal definitely worth taking.

CHEATERS and THIEVES

Rob sat between Thom and Hashemi in the newsroom. The laptop screen displayed all sixteen of the security cameras, and so far, no one had come close to heading their way. Megan sat across from him, her eyes glued to her phone, her fingernails tapping against the table. Rob could never figure out why a girl as pretty as Megan hung out with a geek like Hashemi. She had even quit the cheerleading squad to spend more time with him — to build a stupid robot. That was like cashing in a winning lottery ticket for a pocketful of rusted pennies.

"How's it going down there?" Bradley asked. Rob jumped. He was still getting used to the earpiece.

"Still waiting," Jackson said. He remained against the doorjamb, and was much too calm and cool for Rob's liking.

"Want me to come down?" Bradley asked.

Jackson leaned out of the door, peered down the hallway toward Mrs. Clark's room, then shook his head. "No. I need you to stay by that frame. We're going to have to move quickly if Serena doesn't fall for the survey." He turned to Hashemi. "Let us know as soon as you see her head pop out of that door."

Hashemi nodded. "Understood."

"Why are we wasting so much time?" Rob asked. "We could have already been in and out by now."

"As much as I hate admitting it, you're probably right," Jackson said. "But too much time has passed at this point. Now we're stuck waiting."

"This is a trick, isn't it?" Rob popped his knuckles. "You want Serena to catch us, don't you?"

Jackson groaned. "Do you even listen to the words coming out of your mouth? That makes no sense. Of course I don't want Serena to catch us," he said. "You think Kelsey has it bad for *you*? Try walking in my shoes."

Hashemi pushed his glasses up the bridge of his nose. "We *have* lost a lot of time, Jackson."

"I know, I know." Jackson glanced down the hallway. "Bradley's getting a bit keyed up. If we don't —"

"*Qapla'!*" Megan yelled, jumping up from the table.

Thom and Rob stood as well. "What is it?" Thom asked. "What's wrong?"

"She's just speaking Klingon," Hashemi said. "It means 'success.'"

"Serena took the bait — she's taking the survey," Megan said. "Also, Samuel says that you owe him five bucks, Jackson." She frowned at the screen for a second before breaking into a grin. "He also said you can keep the money if you admit you're scared to kiss —"

"Okay, let's go," Jackson said, slapping his hands

together and pushing off the doorjamb. "We don't want to waste time."

Bradley entered the newsroom. "So now what?" he asked.

"Now Rob and Thom go steal the test," Jackson said. He took the keys from Bradley, then tossed them to Rob. "You two wanted to tag along to get the test so badly . . . Now's your chance."

Rob puffed out his chest. "Come on, Thom."

"Remember, get in and get out," Jackson said as Rob and Thom walked toward the door. "We've got less than ten minutes."

Rob waved his arm dismissively as they entered the hallway. Thom opened his mouth to speak, but Rob shook his head. He pointed to the microphone clipped underneath his collar. *Those idiots are still listening in*, he mouthed.

Thom nodded and smiled. *Idiots*, he mouthed back.

Rob opened the door to Mrs. Clark's room and made a beeline for the file cabinet. He was just unlocking it when he heard someone approaching. He spun around to see Bradley entering the room.

"What are you doing here?" he asked.

"I wanted to make sure you didn't need help."

"We can handle this, kid," Rob said. He hated cocky sixth graders like Bradley. Sixth graders weren't supposed to be popular. They were supposed to wait their turn like everyone else. But by having a few of the right friends — namely, Jackson Greene — Bradley had shot up the social food chain.

Rob and Thom finally found the test. "Thom, grab your phone and take a picture of it."

"I don't have my phone," Thom replied. "I left it in my bag."

"Me too," Rob said. Jackson had ordered everyone to remove anything nonessential from their pockets before their sprint down the hallway. They'd left their personal phones, their pencils — everything — in their book bags, which were back in the gym.

Bradley took a step forward and pulled a pen from his pocket. "Here, use this —"

"Like I said, we've got it," Rob snapped. He grabbed one of Mrs. Clark's test pens and a loose sheet of printer paper from the file cabinet. "Don't take it personally, kid," he said. "But we don't trust you."

"Fine. Just hurry," Bradley said. "Serena won't be taking that survey forever."

Rob nudged Thom. "You call out the answers. I'll write."

Once they compiled the answers and double-checked them, Rob and Thom tossed the keys to Bradley and exited the room.

Jackson was standing in the hall. "Did you get it?" he asked, his hand tightly curled around the PVC stand outside of Mrs. Clark's room. "Are you sure it was the right test? There are a lot of papers in that file cabinet."

Rob waved the paper and grinned. "Does the high-and-mighty Jackson Greene want to see the answers?"

"No thanks," Jackson said, turning away.

"So now what?" Rob asked. "How are you going to remove the tablets and stands? Serena's going to know something's up if we turn off the cameras again."

Jackson smiled. "Exactly."

POOR service

Serena had just finished question eight of the incredibly long survey when the cameras died again.

"Are you guys still working on our system?" she asked the technician. "The cameras blacked out."

"That's odd," he said. "Let me check —"

The line went silent.

Serena tapped a few buttons, hoping that she'd been placed on hold. But when she heard the dial tone, she quickly punched in the phone number the technician had left her.

"Hello, you've reached the cell phone of Alex Westing. If you're calling in reference to apartment 3D in Sunset Towers, please ring me on my office phone at —"

Serena hung up.

It had to be Jackson.

She scooped the keys from the desk and rushed out of the room. As she jogged toward the social studies wing, she speed-dialed Mr. James. Her sister had teased her about saving his number in her phone that morning, but now she was glad she'd done it. "Mr. James, can you meet me in the newsroom?" she asked.

"Serena? Is that you? What's wrong?"

"The cameras are off. It's Jackson. He's in the newsroom. Or at least, he's supposed to be there. That's where I last saw him."

"Be there in a second," he said.

She ended the call and picked up her pace. Instead of knocking on the door to the newsroom, she barged right in. Jackson and Bradley sat at a large table covered with laptops and newspaper layouts. In the corner, Hashemi held up a tablet and was recording Megan talking in front of a blank wall. Rob and Thom stood by the window, whispering to each other.

"Hi, Serena." Jackson rose from a table and tucked his pencil behind his ear. "What brings you here?"

"You're up to something," she said. "Admit it."

"Up to what?" He straightened his tie. "We're finalizing the story about the game."

Serena crossed her arms. "But the game isn't over."

Megan motioned for Hashemi to stop recording. "Clearly you didn't see the score. And thanks for barging in and messing up my video."

"Where's Charlie?" Serena asked. "He's the editor, right? Isn't he supposed to be here?"

"I think he went to see Gaby play," Jackson said. "Which is where I should be."

Mr. James entered the room. "What's the problem here?"

"They're up to something," Serena said. "I know it."

She leaned close to Mr. James and covered her mouth. "Maybe we should check Mrs. Clark's room."

"Already did. It's locked up tight," he said. Then he looked at the others. "There sure are a lot of you in here. Where's your advisor?"

"Mr. Portillo couldn't stay after school, but he said we could meet without him," Bradley said. "You can ask him yourself."

Serena frowned at Rob and Thom as they walked toward her. "When did you two join the newspaper staff?"

"Yesterday," Rob mumbled.

Jackson slapped him on the back, and Rob jerked forward. "Membership drive. We're thinking about adding a video component to the newspaper."

Mr. James rubbed his chin. "Mr. Gonzales let you out of the gym?"

Jackson nodded. "We have passes and everything. Want to see them?"

He shook his head. "No, I don't think —"

"Mr. James!" Serena said.

"No, I don't need to see them," he continued. "But I think y'all should head on home. The story can wait until tomorrow."

While Jackson, Megan, Bradley, and Hashemi cleaned off the table and packed up their bags, Rob and Thom shot out of the room.

"It's impossible to get good help nowadays," Jackson said.

Serena and Mr. James followed Jackson and the crew into the hallway. Jackson locked the office door, then slipped the key into his pocket. "Don't worry, it's Charlie's key. He let me borrow it."

As Jackson and the others walked toward the exit, Serena looked up at the video camera aimed at the newsroom. The light was on — it was working again. Then she noticed the recycling bin sitting directly underneath it. She lifted the lid.

"What's this?" she asked.

Jackson paused only for a second before continuing to walk.

"Jackson! I'm talking to you —"

"It's PVC pipe," Mr. James said. "Probably for some class exercise."

"But they just emptied the bins," she said. "I saw them wheeling in new ones this afternoon."

"Serena, it's time to go," Mr. James said. He placed his hand on her shoulder, softly but firmly. "Come on and collect your books."

As they returned to the security room, Serena tried to explain everything that had happened. "I promise, Mr. James, the cameras went off. Twice. And I was talking to some guy from KRX, except I don't think he was really from the security company —"

"Serena, you've been a big help. Honestly, I mean that." Mr. James unlocked the door. "But maybe you've watched enough video feeds this week. All that staring at the monitor and such can't be good for the brain, you know."

Even though she could tell Mr. James wasn't happy, he was smiling. It was pained, but it was a smile.

Serena picked up her book bag. "Look at the video. The cameras were off-line."

"I will. Tomorrow." He guided her toward the door. "Good night, Serena. And thanks again for helping out."

"Promise you'll check —"

Serena stopped. There was no use in talking to a closed door.

a NEW Deal

Charlie was waiting for the crew when they reached Hashemi's shed. "Did you finish the story?" he asked. "We print tomorrow morning."

"The story was done before the game even started," Jackson said. "Though after today, I think I'm out of the news business."

Charlie picked up a brown cardboard box. "Me and my back say you got the good end of the deal."

They entered the shed, then Charlie placed the box on the worktable. "One Pikachu, as promised."

"And the MATE?" Hashemi asked.

"Worked like a charm," he said. "No issues shutting off the cameras and sneaking in." Charlie sat down. "You know, for projects that are always in progress, your inventions usually work pretty well."

Megan opened her laptop. "Haven't you guys realized — a beta device for Hashemi is like a third-generation device for normal people?" She logged onto her machine. "Except when it comes to the RhinoBot."

"I'll get that ram to work! Eventually."

"Simmer down, Hash. She's joking." Jackson frowned as he studied Megan. "I think."

"Where's Gaby?" Bradley asked.

"She'll be here soon," Charlie said. "Mom took her to dinner. The girls won by eight points. Gaby had a double-double."

"I really wish I'd been at that game," Jackson said.

"Mom taped it, since Dad wasn't able to make it either," Charlie said. "He's going to watch it this weekend. Mom said you're welcome to come over and watch it with him."

"I'll, um, keep that in mind." Jackson loosened his tie. "Okay, we have some time to kill before Victor gets here. Let's not waste it."

Most of the crew settled around the worktable and studied for their American history exam. Bradley worked on an assignment for math class. Megan tinkered with her hacking program.

An hour later, there was a knock on the door. "It's me," Victor called from outside. "Let us in."

Jackson looked at the others, then closed his textbook. "It's unlocked."

Victor entered the shed, followed by Rob and Thom. Hashemi had redecorated in the four months since he'd last been here, Victor noticed. But he still had those stupid *Star Trek* dolls all over the place.

"You brought company," Jackson said. "Did you also bring the hard drive?"

"Nice try, Jackson." Victor turned to Bradley. "The

next time you create a disappearing ink, make sure it lasts longer than an hour."

Jackson pursed his lips together and glanced at Bradley. "An hour?"

Bradley shrugged. "I didn't expect them to write the answers on paper. I thought they'd write on their skin."

"It was a smart plan," Victor continued. "A nice countermove. When did you replace the pens in Mrs. Clark's file cabinet? Last week?"

Jackson cracked a smile. "I wish I could claim we swapped out the pens that far in advance, but honestly, we replaced them a few minutes before Rob and Thom went in."

"When?" Thom said. "You were with us."

"But I wasn't," Bradley said.

Thom shook his head. "Jackson was talking to you the entire time. He was looking at you while he talked to you."

"Are you sure I was looking at Bradley when I was leaning out the doorway? Or was I checking to see if he'd already snuck into Mrs. Clark's room?"

"So what are you proposing? A trade?" Victor asked. "I know you have a copy of the answers."

Bradley nodded. "I wrote them down when I returned the regular pens to the file cabinet, after Rob and Thom left the room."

"Great. Hand them over," Thom said.

Charlie stepped forward. "Sure. As soon as you hand over that doctored video."

"Before you give us the answers? No way," Victor said.

Jackson twirled his pencil. "Then we have a stalemate."

"Don't forget who has the video of you all breaking into the school," Rob said.

"*Doctored* video," Jackson said. "But you know, we have a video of our own. Megan, if you don't mind . . ."

Megan had already pulled up the video on the MATE. She angled it so Victor, Rob, Thom, and Bradley could see the screen. Rob and Thom popped into view, the keys to Mrs. Clark's room clearly in Rob's grasp. They unlocked the door and entered the room.

"So what?" Rob's voice was wavering. "If you got us on video, then you also caught Bradley —"

He stopped talking. The screen had gone blank.

"Technical difficulties," Megan said. "You know how fickle video technology can be."

Thom frowned as he squinted at the tablet. "But how —"

"Wait, there's more," Megan said. "Part two."

Sure enough, the video switched back on, and a few seconds later, Rob and Thom exited the room. Then Rob looked up, said something to someone offscreen, and waved a piece of paper with the test answers in front of the camera.

Megan shut off the tablet and handed it to Jackson.

"The MATEs were recording the whole time," Hashemi said happily.

"And what's better than a fake video, Charlie?" Jackson asked.

Charlie winked. "A real one."

213

Victor couldn't help but smile. This was even better than chess. Jackson Greene really was one of the best strategists he'd ever met. He'd be much better off using his talents as part of the Chess Team instead of wasting his time with the Botany Club.

"Just so you know, I asked Kayla to look into those watches to make sure there weren't any nasty surprises embedded in them," Victor said. "Surprise, surprise . . . Those watches were designed to stop working come first period."

"Hm . . . Didn't see that one coming," Megan mumbled.

"She's already working on removing all the software and wiping the watches clean." He pulled out his pocket watch and popped it open, even though he didn't need to check the time. "We'll also be getting some new, longer-lasting UV ink. We'd hate for our answers to disappear again."

Jackson turned to Charlie. "Plan D?"

Charlie nodded. "Plan D."

"And what exactly is plan D?" Victor asked.

"It's the one where we call a truce," Jackson said. "Look, I don't care what you guys do anymore. If you want to cheat, fine. We won't rat. We only want to clear our names." He stood up from the table. "We can make the exchange tomorrow. Six forty-five. At the picnic tables at school. The doctored video for the answers."

Thom shook his head. "But how will we know that you won't try to double-cross us? You might try to catch us on video again and —"

"I'll be right there with you. I'll even bring Hash —

he'll prove that the cameras won't be recording," Jackson said. "So do we have a deal or what?"

Victor sneered at Jackson's outstretched hand, but he shook it. "Deal," he said.

After Victor, Rob, and Thom left, Charlie opened up his textbook. "Well, that was unpleasant."

"And easy," Jackson said. "He agreed way too quickly." He looked at Hashemi. "Did you get what you need?"

Hashemi nodded as he took the MATE from Megan. "We'll be ready come tomorrow morning."

Megan blew a strand of hair from her face. "I can't believe Kayla found the virus in my program. *In a day.*"

"I told you she was smart," Hashemi said as he launched an app on the MATE. He tapped on the screen a few times, then nodded. "Victor was correct. Kayla has already wiped the software from two of the watches, and she's in the process of formatting the third."

"I hope she was up all night searching through the code," Megan said.

Bradley glanced over Hashemi's shoulder. "I have to admit, that's a pretty fancy tablet."

Hashemi beamed. "The MATE is the most technologically astute, progressive —"

"Hash, we don't need the commercial," Jackson said before pulling out his notebook. "Everyone okay with plan D?"

They all nodded.

"Good," Jackson said. "Any other comments?"

Charlie cleared his throat. "You should have let me call it the Zugzwang."

THE **WHITE ELEPHANT** EXCHANGE

The next morning, Jackson and Hashemi sat at the picnic table behind the school and watched as Victor, Rob, and Thom crept along the edge of the parking lot. The sun had barely risen above the tree line, and except for Mr. Hutton's old red pickup, the parking lot was empty. Still, they refused to walk normally, instead crouching close to the ground.

"They look like hermit crabs," Hashemi said.

"Yeah. If hermit crabs got arthritis and liked to cheat on tests." Jackson eyed the MATE in Hashemi's hands. "You might as well bring up the cameras. That's the first thing Victor's going to want to see."

Sure enough, as soon as Victor reached the table, he said, "Pull up the cameras."

"Told you," Jackson mumbled as Hashemi passed the MATE to Victor. "Satisfied?" he asked Victor.

"For now." Victor returned the tablet to Hashemi. "Where's the video of Rob and Thom?"

Jackson pulled a DVD from his book bag. "Voila."

"What about the answers to the test?" Rob asked.

"Duh, they're on the video," Jackson said.

"And how exactly are we supposed to bring that up?" Rob asked.

"You're welcome to open the video using one of the computers in the library," Jackson replied.

"I knew you'd try to trick us!" Victor said.

"Calm down," Jackson said as he pulled two folded pieces of paper from his pocket. "Bradley not only wrote down the answers, he also printed out a screenshot of Rob coming out of Mrs. Clark's room."

Victor took the papers and opened them. Rob had waved the answers at the MATE, but even with an extreme zoom, Victor could read only half of the answers clutched in Rob's hand. He quickly checked the first ten letters against the other sheet. They matched.

"How do I know that you didn't give us fake answers?"

"Why do you care?" Jackson asked. "You have a B going into the final, right?"

Victor didn't reply as he passed the paper to Rob. "Write lightly — you don't want Mrs. Clark to be able to see the ink from her desk." Then he opened his book bag, pulled out the hard drive, and handed it to Jackson. "You're right — I don't *have* to cheat. But why get a B when you can get an A?"

Jackson shook his head. "Stop talking and get to writing." He rose from the table. "And don't worry — Hash'll stay here until you're finished. That way, you'll know we didn't move the cameras to record you."

"Where are you going?" Victor asked quickly.

"There's no way I'm bringing this hard drive into the school building with me," he said. "I'm going to hide it in the toolshed in the garden."

Victor looked across the parking lot toward the garden and toolshed. "Oh, okay," he said. "That makes sense."

Jackson tucked the hard drive underneath his arm. "As soon as I hide it, Hash is going to turn a camera toward the toolshed. So don't get any ideas about sneaking in there to steal it back."

"Don't worry," Victor said, his grin as wide as his face. "Going into that garden is the last thing I plan to do."

ONE BRIGHT SPOT
IN THE DAY

There were many things about teaching that Johanna Clark would miss, but end-of-semester grading would not be one of them. Every year, she tried to give her students (and herself) an out through her practice exam. Every year, they disappointed her.

As she walked down the hallway toward her classroom, she was glad that that seventh grader, Serena Bianchi, wasn't there to ambush her. Every day this week, Serena had hunted her down — in her classroom, in the teacher's lounge, and once outside her bathroom stall — and questioned her about her students and her exam. Even Dr. Kelsey didn't ask so many questions, and he had perfected the art of micromanagement.

She unlocked the door and flipped on the light.

"Hm," she mumbled. "How about that."

a TRAIL OF CHEESE

Serena didn't ride to school with her sister on Friday morning. She didn't have any reason to go early anymore, as she was sure Mr. James didn't want her monitoring the security video. She had actually thought about skipping school, but her mother wouldn't let her. So she decided to walk.

She arrived at school a few minutes before homeroom. Her usual bench was overrun with noisy eighth graders. She started to head to the library but stopped when she saw Lincoln cutting through the crowd toward her.

"Where have you been?" he asked. "Mr. James and I have been looking for you."

"Is he still mad at me?"

"Mr. James wasn't upset." Then Lincoln shrugged. "Well, maybe a little — you can be a bit intense. But he finally looked at the video, and you were right — the cameras were shut off yesterday. *Twice.* And you definitely received a bogus call."

"It doesn't matter," she said. "They got away with it. I know they somehow got into Mrs. Clark's room and stole that test. And I couldn't stop them."

Lincoln led her to a quiet corner. "Serena, how many times do I have to tell you — it's not our job to police the school."

"That's easy for you to say. I'm the one who was duped."

"You think you're the only person who's been tricked by the Infamous Jackson Greene?"

"So you finally believe that Jackson is involved?"

"Well, duh," Lincoln said. "I've always believed that Jackson had his hand in this. I just don't know what 'this' is."

"It's obvious. He's stealing the American history exam. It's the only thing that connects him, Charlie, Victor, Rob, and Thom."

Lincoln was already shaking his head. "Jackson's a lot of things, but he's not a cheater." He looked across the atrium. Victor Cho stood by the vending machines, staring at the back of his hand. "But Victor . . ."

"Is Victor smart enough to pull off something like this?"

"He probably thinks he is," Lincoln said. "You should go and talk to him."

"Why?"

"Because he stopped me in the hallway," Lincoln said. "It turns out that Mr. James and I weren't the only people looking for you this morning."

UNDER THE SPOTLIGHT

While Victor told Serena about the suspicious activity he'd seen in the garden that morning, especially around the toolshed, Rob entered the last stall in the first floor boys' bathroom. He hated this stall — it was dark and dirty and smelled like his baby brother's diaper pail — but it was the most private place in the school.

He pressed the button on his watch and looked at the answers on the back of his hand. Once he practiced a few different techniques for pressing the button while innocently looking at the back of his hand, he committed the first five answers to memory. He figured he'd only have to check his watch eight or nine times during the exam. Maybe even less if he actually knew some of the answers.

Of course, he would have had a better shot at knowing the answers if he had truly studied, but that hadn't seemed necessary until last night, when it looked like Victor's plan might not work. And by then it seemed pointless to even try to prepare.

He checked the time, then rushed to class. He bumped into Jackson on the way to his desk, accidentally on purpose, then slid into his seat as the bell rang.

Mrs. Clark didn't waste time with small talk. She ordered the students to put away their study materials, then walked through each row, handing out the fifty-question exam and test pens.

Rob bent over his test. He felt proud of himself — he remembered four of the first five answers, and even knew two additional ones after that.

Then he had to name the last major battle of the Revolutionary War.

He glanced toward the front of the room. Once he was sure that Mrs. Clark wasn't looking at him, he pressed the small button on his watch. Light beamed out through the side of its case, but he couldn't read the letters on his hand.

I must not have pressed it hard enough, he thought. He pressed the button again. He even cupped his right hand a little tighter around the back of his left, trying to cast a shadow.

Is that a B? Or a D? The writing is too light to —

"Hands above your desk!"

Rob jerked his hand away from his watch. Then he realized that Mrs. Clark was talking to Thom, not him.

Was Thom having trouble reading the test answers as well? He must have tried to put his hands underneath his desk to make the answers darker.

Rob looked at the ceiling. He hadn't noticed it before, but . . .

He raised his hand and cleared his throat.

Mrs. Clark eyed him. "Is there a problem?" Her voice could cut through brick.

"It seems a little . . . bright in here," Rob said.

She nodded. "I noticed that this morning. Mr. Hutton finally replaced my fluorescent lights with newer, stronger bulbs. I've only been complaining about it for twelve years." Her face turned stern. "Now, back to the test."

Rob sighed, picked up his pen, and started guessing.

By the time he reached the midpoint of the exam, he knew that finishing the test was pointless. There was no way he was going to pass. He and Thom would be right back here for summer school.

And then, when Rob thought his day couldn't get any worse, Becca Simpson, the first period office helper, entered the room.

a RAT WITH a WATCH IS STILL a RAT

Victor sat in algebra, ignoring his teacher as she droned on and on about slopes and inequalities. He wished he were sitting next to a window. He wanted to see Serena visit the toolshed and retrieve the hard drive.

He'd always assumed that Jackson would try to double-cross him at some point. So Victor had decided to take the offensive. To be proactive. To turn Jackson in before Jackson could beat him to it. Sure, that would mean he couldn't blackmail Jackson for the rest of the school year, but he'd still have the answers to the test, and he would have humiliated Jackson Greene. Wanting more would have been greedy.

The bell finally rang, and he slipped out of his desk, eager to get to American history. He looked at the back of his hand. No, he didn't need to cheat, but there was nothing wrong with a little insurance.

Mr. James was waiting outside of Mrs. Clark's room. "Victor, you need to come with me."

Victor frowned as he noticed Jackson standing behind Mr. James. Jackson's silly tie was pulled slightly to the left — why couldn't he wear it the correct way? — and he sported a small smirk.

"Is there a problem?" Victor asked, trying to keep his voice steady.

"Just . . . come with me," Mr. James said. "We have a few details we need to clear up."

Victor quickly glanced in Mrs. Clark's classroom.

"Looking for someone?" Jackson asked. "Seems like there was an issue with a couple of our classmates."

Victor placed his hands behind his back, as if Mr. James could see the invisible ink on his skin. "I still don't understand —"

"That's why we're all going to the security room," Mr. James said. "Best to discuss this as a group."

They arrived at the room to find Dr. Kelsey and Serena huddled around the desk. "Finally. Now we can get some real answers," Dr. Kelsey said.

Victor held back as the others entered the room. "But I have a test."

"Mr. Cho, the last thing you need to worry about is your exam," he said. "Now come in and shut the door."

Victor shuffled forward a few steps, pulling the door closed behind him.

"Serena was kind enough to retrieve the NVR hard drive that you said you saw Jackson place in the toolshed," Dr. Kelsey said, waving toward the box on the desk. "Are you sure you didn't see anyone else entering the shed?"

Victor set his jaw and nodded at Jackson. "Just him."

"But you and Rob and Thom have been in the shed before," Serena said. "I've seen you there. And unlike Jackson, you aren't members of the Botany Club."

Victor crossed his arms. "That's the stolen hard drive, right? Did you all even look at it?"

"Oh, we looked at it," Dr. Kelsey said. "Most of the drive has been erased, but we could access one video." He nodded to Serena, and she started the video — of Rob and Thom sneaking into Mrs. Clark's room.

Dr. Kelsey turned back toward the boys once it ended. "Rob and Thom are in my office now. According to them, you two are the ones behind it all." He tapped his fingers on the desk. "Either of you have anything to say about that?"

"I have no idea what they're talking about," Jackson said. Then he turned to Victor and smiled.

Victor balled his hands into fists. "Well, it's obvious, isn't it? They tried to rope me into their plan, but I said no. I'm not a cheater." He pointed to Jackson. "But everyone knows that Jackson Greene is a —"

Before he could finish, the lights shut off, pitching the room into darkness.

"What happened?" Dr. Kelsey spun around. "Did the power go out?"

"The monitor is still on," Serena said. "It must be . . ."

She trailed off as a small lamp on the bookshelf hummed to life. The lamp was angled so almost all of the room was cast in its neon-blue light.

"What in the world?" Mr. James scratched his jaw. "What is that?"

"Wait . . ." Dr. Kelsey took a step toward Victor. "What's that on your hand?" He grabbed Victor's arm and yanked him over to the lamp. "Are those . . . Are those test answers?"

Victor stared at his hand. "I don't — I don't —"

"Serena, pull up that video again," Dr. Kelsey said.

"Already on it," she said as she rewound the video. She froze it at the spot where Rob flashed the test at the camera. "The first four answers are A, D, C, A."

"What do you know? A match." Dr. Kelsey turned to Jackson. "Let's see them."

Jackson held up his hands, showing off his bare brown skin. "I'm happy to roll up my sleeves as well if you'd like."

Before Dr. Kelsey could respond, the NVR started beeping. Then both Mr. James's and Dr. Kelsey's phones began beeping and buzzing.

Mr. James punched in his PIN. "According to this, someone has tried to access the system remotely," he said, his face close to the phone.

The phone in the security office rang, and Dr. Kelsey picked it up before Serena could grab it. "Yes," he said into the receiver. "I see." Another pause. "Yes, we just received that message." One more pause. "Okay, thank you."

He hung up the phone. "That was the security company. They're tracing the access point now — they should be able to pinpoint the exact location where someone tried to log in."

"I knew someone was trying to hack the system!" Serena said, banging on the desk.

"They're still running their diagnostic, but so far, they've been able to determine that another NVR is remotely tied to our system. They're going to pull the serial number from the device and use that to trace the billing statement." Dr. Kelsey looked at Jackson and Victor. "Are you sure there's nothing else you want to tell me?"

Jackson straightened his tie. "Like I said before, I have no idea what any of this is about." He turned to Victor. "What about you?"

Victor let out a deep, long sigh. "I think it's time I called my parents."

IT Takes a THIEF . . .

Thirty minutes after school ended, Serena sat on a bench outside the main building, staring at the street. The entire day had been a blur. She had won. She had caught the cheaters. She had proved that someone was indeed trying to steal Mrs. Clark's test.

But it wasn't Jackson Greene. She had been sure — positive — that he and his crew were the cheaters. How could she have been so wrong?

Maybe she should volunteer to be an office helper. She sure seemed good at jumping through hoops for Dr. Kelsey. And she certainly wasn't cut out for the Honor Board.

She was still sitting on the bench, watching cars pass the school, when Lincoln dropped onto the seat beside her.

"Got a few minutes?" he asked.

She shook her head. "My sister will be here soon."

"It won't kill her to wait for you." He stood, then held his hand out to her. "Come on. I promise it'll be worth it."

She frowned, but allowed him to help her to her feet. "I thought you'd be mad at me," she said. "I was wrong about Jackson."

He chuckled. "I don't know if I'd use the word *wrong*," he said. "Maybe . . . misguided."

"That makes no sense," she said. They stopped at the entrance to the social studies hallway. "We can't go down there. We don't have a meeting today, and we don't have a pass."

"Serena, for once, let's bend the rules a little." He opened the door, and after a second, she slipped into the hallway.

She thought they were headed to Mr. Pritchard's room, or even Mrs. Clark's room, but instead they stopped at the newsroom. Charlie, Hashemi, Megan, and Bradley looked up as Lincoln opened the door.

"I knew you guys were behind it!" Serena yelled.

Charlie rolled his eyes. "Are you sure we have to explain it to her?"

"It's either that or have her tailing you for the rest of the year," Lincoln replied.

"Hold on." Megan raised her arms. "Want to check our hands again before we start?"

Serena tightened her grip on her book bag straps. She had personally checked the hands of each member of Gang Greene after discovering the ink on Victor. Rob and Thom had smudges of ink on their hands as well, although it appeared that they'd tried to lick the answers off while they were waiting in Dr. Kelsey's office.

"So tell me the truth," she said to Charlie. "Did you steal the test?"

"Maybe we should back up," Charlie said. "The only reason we got into this mess in the first place is because Victor was trying to blackmail us. He's the one who flooded the school and stole the hard drive."

"Rob and Thom confessed," Lincoln said.

"They also said that you helped them steal the test, and then you double-crossed them," Serena said.

Charlie smiled. "Jackson never planned to let those guys cheat on the test. But the only way to clear our names was to catch them in the act of stealing it."

"So you admit it," Serena said. "You did steal it."

"We helped *Rob and Thom* steal it," Charlie said. "There's a difference."

"That's quite a technicality."

"But it's true. Thanks to Megan and Bradley, the rest of us were able to avoid looking at any of the test answers." Charlie rose from his chair. "We originally planned for Rob and Thom to use disappearing UV ink during the test — the answers would fade away before they even sat down at their desks. Once we figured out what Victor was really up to, we came up with a new plan to have the UV watches short-circuit during first period, in the middle of the exam. But we knew that Victor would ask Kayla Hall, his tech guru —"

"Guru? Ha!" Megan said.

Charlie sighed. "That he would get Kayla, his . . . whatever . . . to check the watches."

"Once Kayla connected the watches to her desktop

and checked the code, we realized it would only be a matter of time before she found the program we'd installed to shut down the UV light," Hashemi said. "However, while she was deleting that software, we were able to remotely upload a program to her desktop to crack her password."

"That only took twelve hours to crack, thank you very much," Megan added.

"That allowed us to access her computer and the NVR that Victor purchased for her, and initiate the log-in to the school's security system," Charlie said. "That's what happened while you were in the security room this morning. Which, of course, you realized when all the alerts started going off."

"But how?" Serena let her book bag slide to the ground. "You all were in class."

Hashemi pulled out the MATE. "The Most Awesome Tablet Ever, Version Four, is the most technically astute, progressive —"

"Hashemi!" Charlie, Bradley, and Megan yelled at the same time.

He cleared his throat. "Megan and I developed a voice-activated program and script that would automatically access Kayla's computer, her NVR, and the lamps in the security office via the MATE," he said. "Charlie placed a stripped-down version of the MATE and the UV lamp in the security office yesterday afternoon, then plugged the lamp into a special dongle that connected it to our system. After that, all it needed was a voice command to start the sequence."

"Jackson activated it?" Serena asked.

"No, Victor did," Hashemi said. "When he said Jackson's name."

"We're not rats," Charlie said. "But we weren't going to stop Victor from ratting on himself."

"But wait . . . When did you get into the security room yesterday?" she asked. "I was there the entire time. . . ."

"Except when we turned off the cameras so you'd rush to the other side of the school," Bradley said. "Charlie was hiding in the storage closet —"

"Where I also stashed a box of high-powered fluorescent lights," Charlie said, "and added a work order for Mr. Hutton to install them in Mrs. Clark's room."

"Fluorescent lights?" Serena asked. "What does that have to do with anything?"

"Again, remember, we never planned to let Rob, Thom, and Victor cheat on the test," Charlie said. "Bradley tricked Rob and Thom into using disappearing ink when they wrote down the answers in the first place so they wouldn't be able to memorize them overnight, and then we created a room so bright that they weren't able to read the writing on their hands with the UV watches. We figured that would be enough to ensure that they didn't cheat."

Serena glanced at the window. Her sister was probably outside, but she could wait all day for all Serena cared. She needed more answers.

"So back to the video of Rob and Thom sneaking into Mrs. Clark's room. How did you get that onto the hard drive?" She'd checked the serial numbers — it really was the same hard drive that had been stolen two weeks ago.

"Well, Victor had Kayla doctor the video of Rob and Thom flooding the school so it looked like all of us did it," Charlie said. "Jackson and Victor came to an agreement — the doctored video for the test answers. And Victor wasn't lying — Jackson really did place the hard drive in the shed. But Victor didn't know that Megan was also in the shed, waiting to replace the doctored video with the video of Rob and Thom."

Serena slumped against a desk. "How did you guys even pull this off?"

"We got a little help from the Environmental Action Team, and I was able to convince the *Herald* staff to let me borrow the newsroom for a while." Charlie ran his fingers through his hair. "And . . . we needed an Isabel Lahiri."

Serena blinked. "A who?"

"Didn't you ever watch *Ocean's Twelve*? It's not as good as the first and third movies in the series, but —"

"Maybe you should get on with the explanation," Lincoln said.

"Okay. Sure," Charlie said. "We needed someone who Mr. James and Dr. Kelsey would trust to review the video. Someone who would follow up on the leads and figure out that Victor, Rob, and Thom were involved as well. Someone who would be relentless in pursuing 'justice' . . . even if it meant making a deal with Keith Sinclair so he could buy a new hard drive for the school."

"You're talking about me," Serena said. "You've been playing me the entire time."

"Well, not the *entire* time," Bradley said. "Just from the point where you saw everyone in the garden, after Charlie told Jackson how you'd been keeping tabs on us."

Serena didn't know whether to be amazed or disgusted. "How did you even know I'd follow up? That I'd fall for it?"

"Well, the Environmental Action Team weren't our only silent partners," Charlie said.

Serena followed Charlie's gaze until she landed on Lincoln. "You were in on this as well?"

Lincoln shrugged. "You were always dead set on trying to catch Jackson. I just did a little nudging . . . making sure you stayed on the right path."

"So I'd make a fool of myself."

"No. So you'd catch the right person." Lincoln looked back at Gang Greene. "What can I say? Sometimes it takes a thief to catch a cheat."

"So why are you telling me all this?" she asked. "I could turn you all in, you know."

Charlie grinned. "Well, first — you won't turn us in. You don't have any evidence except for a tablet tucked away in a dusty corner of the security room — a tablet that has already been remotely wiped and reformatted."

"MATE, Version One," Hashemi mumbled. "She served us well."

"And we've already destroyed our copies of the keys to the security room, Mrs. Clark's classroom, and her file cabinet," Bradley said.

"We're telling you because we want you to know we weren't the bad guys here," Megan said. "We were only trying to clear our names, and stop a few cheaters in the process."

"Jackson and his crew really are the good guys," Lincoln said. "If you're going to be Honor Board chair next year, you'd better learn who you can trust around here."

"You think I can be chair?" Serena asked.

"Maybe. You certainly have the drive for it. Let's see how the second semester goes. We need to work on your people skills a bit." Lincoln rubbed his hands together. "So, any more questions?"

Serena looked back at the group. "Where's Jackson?"

They all broke into smiles, but no one spoke.

"Let me guess," Serena said. "The Infamous Jackson Greene has one last job to pull before he rides off into retirement."

"That remains to be seen," Charlie said. "Why? Interested in making a bet?"

FINΛL **EXAM**

While the rest of Gang Greene talked with Serena in the newsroom, Jackson headed down the deserted hallway toward his locker. He had spent the last twenty minutes in the garden, clearing away all the trash and filling it with potted chrysanthemums and tea candles. It had taken almost four months, but he'd finally come up with the perfect plan for kissing Gaby. Now he just had to figure out how to get her outside without tipping her off.

He slowed as he reached his locker — the padlock was missing. Everything inside was as usual, except for a wrapped gift and a tin of mints sitting on top of his books. He grinned as he glanced at the camera pointed toward him, and for a second wondered if Gaby had used it to figure out his combination. Then he shook his head. Out of everyone in the school, Gaby was the last person who needed a camera to open his locker.

He grabbed the gift and the mints and shut his locker, then jogged down the hallway and turned the corner. Sure enough, Gaby stood by her locker. She pulled her hair back from her face and smiled broadly. "If it isn't the Infamous Jackson Greene. Tell me the truth — you loved being back on the job."

"I'm not the one who just broke into an innocent student's locker," he said. "Weren't you scolding me two weeks ago about breaking into Hashemi's shed?"

"A lot can happen in two weeks." Gaby pulled the padlock from her pocket and tossed it to Jackson. Then she nodded at the gift in his hands. "Open it."

He started to peel away the paper. "I think you have this backward. *Your* birthday is on Monday. I'm supposed to be giving *you* a present." He held up the new red leather notebook. "Thanks. I was almost out of pages in my old one."

"Yeah, I know," she said.

He leaned back. "You looked in my notebook?"

"Why, are you worried? It's not like I can decipher your code," she said. "And in case you were wondering, I love Ruth Bader Ginsburg."

Jackson coughed a little. "I wanted to get the Sonia Sotomayor one as well, but it was on back order and —"

"Here's what I really want for my birthday," she said. "I want you to come to my house this weekend. I want you to watch my game with me and my dad. He promised to be on his best behavior."

He gulped as he loosened his tie, but nodded.

"And a nice biography to go with the Chia Pet wouldn't hurt either."

Jackson laughed. "Okay. I'll be busy with Charlie on Sunday, but I'll come by on Saturday afternoon."

"What do you two have going on?"

"Samuel was able to get his hands on a layout of Riggins," he said. "And Bradley has a friend there who coated the keypad lock with UV powder. And we have Megan's password program that she's dying to use again." He shrugged. "What can I say? Charlie's one of my best friends. And it's his birthday too."

"He always gets the good gifts," she mumbled. Then she crunched on something — and Jackson realized he'd never opened his tin of mints.

"Oh, wait . . ." He pulled the tin from his pocket and started to fumble with the clear plastic wrapper.

Gaby reached out and stopped him. "Jackson, enough."

Before he knew it, she stepped forward, placed her arms around his neck, and rose up on her toes.

It was the best two seconds of Jackson's life.

When she pulled back, he realized that his hands had come to rest on her hips. He dropped them, then looked around.

"You've broken, like, a thousand rules this week," she said. "And you're worried about the one against public displays of affection?"

"No . . . I mean, yes . . . I mean —"

She kissed him again.

When they finally pulled away for air, they were both grinning. She dropped her hands and took a few steps back. "Now what?" she asked. "Want to head to Hashemi's?"

Jackson rubbed the back of his neck. "Actually, I was planning to take you to the garden. I had decorated it and everything. It was part of my master plan to . . . you know . . ."

She picked up her book bag and slung it over her shoulder. "Okay, let's go."

"But . . . We already . . . I mean, this was great. I mean, really, really great. There's no point in —"

"Jackson Greene, don't be silly." She looped her arm through his as they started down the hallway. "This was just a practice exam."

TO CATCH A CHEAT CONS

VIZZINI'S CHALLENGE (GABY AND JACKSON SCAMMING ERIC CAAN BY PLAYING A VIDEO GAME WITH BROKEN JOYSTICKS): In *The Princess Bride*, the outlaw Vizzini challenges the Dread Pirate Roberts to a battle of wits. Agreeing, the pirate takes two goblets of wine and laces one with iocane powder, a tasteless, odorless poison. After a brief conversation where Vizzini tries to deduce which goblet holds the poison, they both drink. Vizzini falls dead, and the pirate reveals that both goblets were poisoned — Roberts had spent years building up an immunity to iocane powder. Jackson and Gaby defeated Eric in a similar fashion — by spending their two-week winter break learning how to play *Ultimate Fantasy IV* with broken joysticks.

THE MUTARA NEBULA (THE INSTALLATION OF THE NEW NVR HARD DRIVE): In *Star Trek II: The Wrath of Khan*, the *Enterprise* flees toward the Mutara Nebula while battling an enemy ship with greater speed and firepower. Saavik warns Spock that the static discharge and gas in the nebula will cloud the *Enterprise*'s visuals and render its shields useless. "Sauce for the goose," Spock responds. "The odds will be even."

HAN VAN MEEGEREN (THE MATES): Dutch painter Han van Meegeren dreamed of becoming an established artist, but his work was criticized for being unoriginal and imitative. He managed to turn that criticism to his advantage and emerge as one of the most prominent art forgers of the twentieth century. Van Meegeren duplicated the work of Frans Hals, Johannes Vermeer, and other artists with such cunning skill that renowned art critics claimed his art was the bona fide original.

SUE STORM (THE DISAPPEARING INK): Code-named the Invisible Woman, Sue Storm is a founding member of the Fantastic Four, a superhero group created by Stan Lee and Jack Kirby for Marvel Comics. Storm's powers include the ability to render herself and other objects invisible.

ZUGZWANG (PLAN D): In the game of chess, a Zugzwang refers to a predicament in which one player is forced to move into a disadvantageous situation where any possible move will weaken their position. The smart player who recognizes the coming defeat will choose to play out the game in a manner that forces their opponent into the most debilitating victory possible.

WHITE ELEPHANT (THE EXCHANGE OF THE DOC-TORED VIDEO FOR THE EXAM ANSWERS): In ancient Thailand, the white elephant was considered a sacred animal, and it was a great honor to receive one from a monarch. However, elephants are costly to maintain, and such a precious creature was forbidden to perform profitable labor. Thus, the kings of Siam often bestowed white elephants on courtiers they didn't like in order to ruin them financially.

MR. MAGOO (ROB AND THOM DURING THE EXAM): Cartoon character Quincy Magoo is a wealthy senior citizen with extremely poor eyesight. While Magoo could easily correct his vision with glasses, his stubborn refusal to acknowledge the problem, paired with the poor eyesight itself, often creates comedic situations with disastrous results.

SUPER BOWL XLVII (THE BLACKOUT IN THE SECURITY ROOM): Played on February 3, 2013, in the Superdome in New Orleans, Louisiana, Super Bowl XLVII was a National Football League championship game between the Baltimore Ravens and the San Francisco 49ers. Also nicknamed the Blackout Bowl, play was suspended for more than thirty minutes due to a power outage in the third quarter.

ISABEL LAHIRI (SERENA BIANCHI): In *Ocean's Twelve*, Inspector Isabel Lahiri first confronts Danny Ocean and his crew of con artists as she investigates a botched theft. Driven by professional and personal motivations, Lahiri employs unorthodox (and morally questionable) methods in an attempt to later catch the crew in the act of stealing a Fabergé egg.

BEN KENOBI (LINCOLN MILLER): After the creation of the Galactic Empire, Jedi Master Obi-Wan Kenobi takes the name "Ben" and goes into exile on Tatooine to secretly watch over young Luke Skywalker. Kenobi becomes a mentor to Skywalker and begins to train him in the ways of the Force, all while keeping Luke's true destiny hidden from him.

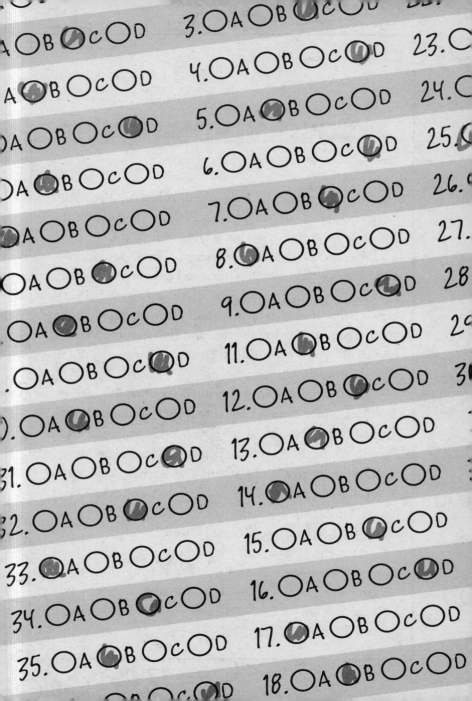

ACKNOWLEDGMENTS

I would like to thank Julie Lake, Brian Yansky, April Lurie, Frances Yansky, and Sean Petrie — you all are the best critique group an author could ask for.

Love and hugs to my agent and friend, Sara Crowe. You have always believed in me, and I am grateful for that.

Cheryl Klein, you are one of the smartest people I know, and I am so, so lucky to call you my editor. Thank you for helping me find the plot and the heart of the story, and thank you for bearing with me as I missed my fair share of deadlines.

To the entire Arthur A. Levine Books/Scholastic team: Arthur Levine, Emily Clement, Kait Feldmann, Weslie Turner, Nina Goffi, Elizabeth Krych, and Saraciea Fennell: I greatly appreciate everything that you do behind the scenes.

I'd like to give special thanks to Rachel Wilson and Mary Winn Heider — this book would not exist if you hadn't forced me to sit down and write it. You two are worth your weight in coffee and gummi bears.

To all the booksellers who support me and Jackson Greene, I am forever in your debt. You changed my life.

And to Crystal, Savannah, and Sydney — thank you for your continued love and support. You are the magic behind the words.

VARIAN JOHNSON

is the author of four previous novels for children and young adults, including *The Great Greene Heist*, which was named an ALSC Notable Book for Children, a *Kirkus Reviews* Best Book of 2014, and a Bank Street College Best Book of the Year. He lives with his wife and daughters near Austin, Texas. You can find him on the web at www.varianjohnson.com and @varianjohnson.

○c ○D   22. ○A ●B ○c ○D   3. ○A ○

○c ○D   23. ○A ○B ○c ●D   4. ○A ○

○c ●D   24. ●A ○B ○c ○D   5. ●A ○

○c ○D   25. ○A ○B ●c ○D   6. ○A ○B

○c ○D   26. ○A ●B ○c ○D   7. ○A ●B

c ○D   27. ●A ○B ○c ○D   8. ●A ○B

c ○D   28. ○A ○B ○c ●D   9. ○A ○B ●

c ○D   29. ○A ○B ●c ○D   11. ○A ○B ○

● ○D   30. ○A ○B ○c ●D   12. ●A ○B ○

○D   31. ○A ●B ○c ○D   13. ○A ●B ○

● D   32. ○A ●B ○c ○D   14. ○A ○B ○

○D   33. ○A ○B ○c ●D   15. ●A ○B ○

○D   34. ●A ○B ○c ○D   16. ○A ○B ●

○D   35. ○A ○B ●c ○D   17. ●A ○B ○

A MYSTERIOUS LETTER

A MISSING FORTUNE

A STRANGE BOY ACROSS THE STREET

AND A COPY OF *THE WESTING GAME*

When Candice Miller finds the letter, she isn't sure she should read it. (It's addressed to her grandmother, after all.) But the letter describes an injustice that happened decades ago. A mystery enfolding the letter-writer. And the fortune that awaits the person who solves the puzzle.

Grandma tried and failed. But now Candice has another chance. With the help of Brandon Jones, the quiet boy across the street, she begins to decipher the clues in the letter. Can they find the fortune and fulfill the letter's promise before the summer ends?

CHECK OUT VARIAN JOHNSON'S
THE PARKER INHERITANCE

ARTHUR A.
LEVINE BOOKS

AALVARIAN3

CHECK OUT JACKSON'S FIRST ADVENTURE!

SAVING THE SCHOOL, ONE CON AT A TIME.

THE GREAT GREENE HEIST

VARIAN JOHNSON

SCHOLASTIC

"A thrilling ride."

—*The New York Times*

When the principal and a bully want to steal the school election, what does it take to do it right? One great candidate, one crack team, and one marvelous mastermind. If they can pull off the biggest con ever, it will go down in history as

THE GREAT GREENE HEIST!

ARTHUR A. LEVINE BOOKS

AALVARIAN